# Hamburger

# Hamburger

DANIEL PERRY

*thistledown press*

Thistledown Press Ltd.
410 2nd Avenue North
Saskatoon, Saskatchewan, S7K 2C3
www.thistledownpress.com

Library and Archives Canada Cataloguing in Publication

Perry, Daniel, 1982–, author
Hamburger / Daniel Perry.

Short stories.
Issued in print and electronic formats.
ISBN 978-1-77187-097-9 (paperback).–ISBN 978-1-77187-098-6 (html).–
ISBN 978-1-77187-099-3 (pdf)

I. Title.
PS8631.E77933H34 2016     C813'.6     C2016-901049-X
C2016-901050-3

Cover and book design by Jackie Forrie
Printed and bound in Canada

Thistledown Press gratefully acknowledges the financial assistance of the Canada Council for the Arts, the Saskatchewan Arts Board, and the Government of Canada through the Canada Book Fund for its publishing program.

# Hamburger

*À l'exploratrice;*
*je n'aurais pas pu savoir*

# CONTENTS

*coarse*

*medium*

*fine*

*coarse*

# Hamburger

*T*he outside wall of the giant corner building is made completely of windows. It's a major intersection, hot July day. Streetcars rattle by half as often as they should. You walk into a place where you sweat more than you do on the pavement — your apartment's also like this — and you smell the smoke, vague and sickly. It's better than the garbage bins lining your street, green ovens baking used diapers and cat litter and fish bones before they serve hungry truck mouths.

People sit inside the glass, steaming like leftovers, dripping condiments, sucking sugar-water through straws. You're still in your work clothes, business casual, button-up and slacks. A messenger bag hangs from your shoulder. Fluorescent lights close in. The counter girl spots you. Her hair is too long under the flat wordmark ball cap, and the humidity cleaves straight lengths apart, loose strands frizzing in-between. She's too short, and her tan's too dark, but at least it's not from a bottle. A soccer player, you think. Eighteen. Maybe less, but she smiles. You fail to return it.

Today marks ten years since your first real date, give or take. You saw her at a bar last week. She didn't even notice you. The first one you loved, still blonde and tall — too tall for you — and still thin, but not *too* thin. She was double the height of the girl

# Hamburger

at the counter, who you'd go to jail for even thinking about. Still. You hope she doesn't see the sweat collecting in your eyebrows, or the deodorant failing in your armpits. They've been wet since ten this morning, stained yellow for a year. That's who you are now.

This joint's mid-level. You can get gorgonzola but it tastes like shit. You mumble when she asks what you want, a six-ounce, not four, not eight. With "regular, boring cheddar." You're uncommitted even to self-deprecation, but you bothered to joke and she caught it. She smiles even wider. There's no name tag. She strikes you as an Emily.

The total's eleven. The cheese was extra. You pay and you stupor your way toward the fountain, where you fill a paper cup with cola you don't want. You sip, it's too syrupy, but you'll drink it all. You load up on ketchup and vinegar and take a vinyl stool at the table by the window. You take the bag off, but your right shoulder still droops lower than your left. You reach in for a book but stop when you see your khaki knees stained, blood and pus oozing from scabs underneath, ground to red pulp, browning like your dinner. They smell just as bad. You fell down drunk last night. Fuck, you hate your job.

The book you pull out is Updike. You've been reading on the subway, three pages a day, flipping back trying to remember what just happened and forgetting to care what comes next. You sip the Coke and mutter, "Fucking windbag." You've read all of Bukowski, and you think you can write like him, but this week both magazines that care in this country rejected you. Really, they both accepted you. You shot yourself in both feet trying to work it out. You didn't know the website said no simultaneous submissions. You only have the internet at work, and you're not allowed to use it. You. Especially you.

# Hamburger

You think you understand why Rabbit ran off. You miss cigarettes, and you wonder, Does Emily smoke? Your girlfriend would throw you out for where both thoughts are headed. You're not sure you care. Your vacation is here and you're going away to write. She doesn't trust that you're coming back. Neither do you. And basically it's because of Emily, who gets that you're reading. She doesn't call the number on your receipt, eighty-six. She sneaks up behind you instead. "Here you go." Almost a whisper. She gently sets your order on the table. Sweet, and smiling ever larger.

You remember the feeling from when you were her age. It lasted a month. You were younger. Your love called it a fling. Now you wonder why she came alone to that bar.

You look up, but only because you're sitting. Emily's so fucking short. Who knows how old she is? Who cares? She sees it in your eyes. The feeling that every move is the wrong one. She's the kind of girl who'll act extra nice if you're down, like everything will be over in a second. You agree, but she's no match for your imagination. You picture the two of you naked on your backs, dead from the bolt's subtle click, painless clunk, as a belt conveys your bodies toward the grinder.

# Fourfather

*T*he summer before I was born, Mom was a tree planter, high on the rocky Canadian Shield in northern Ontario. But she wasn't old or hard like the other women in camp. She'd never had the abortion, the abusive father or the rep as school slut that made the others leave small towns; she was a late bloomer, and at nineteen she barely filled out her T-shirt and dirty overalls. In the faded photo her hair is a pretty blonde, not the few white wisps it is now.

She was with four guys that summer — saplings, all of them, always nicknamed when she talks to me. John was a kind lover but always down on the world. Pretty Paul never said anything important. George rarely said anything at all, even alone with Mom in her tent, and Ringo — "Well, you couldn't be his either," she's always said. "You would have gotten his nose."

The boy next door had loved Mom, too, and after high school they'd had a couple of dates. He moved in with us when I was three, but Mom threw him out before I was old enough to hurt. "I guess he was too eager," she said once. "Too ready for his life to be like all the rest in town history."

But in her hospital bed now, not healing, she squeezes my hand and says, "Pete was best."

# I Think I'll Tell Her Today

*A*ctually, Trevor has two daughters: Gemma, who leaves for school at eight with his wife Molly, and Gabriela, who I take to daycare before I get to their house. He says little while he eats the bacon and over-hard eggs I make him. Blonde Gemma stuffs her mouth with Lucky Charms while Molly clucks her tongue and suggests yogurt and granola. No one listens. She scoops up Gemma and leaves her husband in a T-shirt on the couch with a laptop. He has an office, too, but he's a web designer and works from here most days — way more than Molly knows.

He speaks only once the car's turned onto King Street, when he's sure Molly and Gemma won't be back for something they forgot. He usually says *Come here*, or *I thought she'd never leave*, and I'm usually standing over the dishwasher, emptying it before I put in this morning's pan and bowls. I pretended I didn't want to the first few times — pretended hard, I need this job — but before long we both knew I was acting. I still play the cornered nanny with no choice but to give him what he wants, and I've made him coax me onto the bed and the sofa and one time the kitchen floor, the one I clean every morning. No one would notice if one day I didn't mop, but since my daughter was conceived here I've kept it sparkling.

---

# I Think I'll Tell Her Today

I know, I could quit, just walk away and take a job that pays more than nanny minimum, which of course would be absolutely every job on Earth. The reason could be as simple as "My husband wants me home with Gabriela more", though that would ignore the fact my husband is a fiction. I wear an unpolished, fake gold, pawnshop wedding ring to look suitably poor and happily committed, but it's not like they'll find out; the only time Trevor and Molly invited me to make a foursome was at Canada's Wonderland, when they handed me two-year-old Gemma and three hundred dollars outside of KidZville then went to ride roller coasters. I pocketed one brown bill and we met back in the parking lot at sundown. I had to drive home because Trevor and Molly drank too much at the park's one licensed restaurant, and like teenagers they bickered and whined at each other the whole way. Trevor kept turning backwards to hector Molly, but somehow Gemma, buckled in and clutching her brand new plush Smurfette, didn't rouse beside her. She might have learned to tune them out, but not me. I learned that Trevor goes to the office Thursdays after I leave and stays suspiciously late.

Another time, I found out that Molly's bowling league was actually a pole dancing class. She was trying to surprise him, she said, to put some spice back into things. He just called it trashy. She answered that he was the one sleeping around.

That argument happened while I was in the laundry room, and Gemma in overgrown curls sat in the basket, handing up towels one by one to put in the washer while her parents worked their way up to a screaming match. Molly stormed down the stairs and trundled Gemma off to who knows where. The car started as I threw in the last washcloth and then came Trevor's footsteps. He didn't speak, he just reached under my long skirt and lifted me by the hips onto the washer lid. He pulled my panties to the side and I leaned back, bumping the start button. He used his fingers until the machine filled with water, and when the cycle started he grinned through his goatee and said, *You're such a dirty girl.*

—

I could shame him when I go, too. It wouldn't make the papers, but Molly's friends would all say *I told you so.* On a playdate I heard fat Beth Davies warn her, *The moment you're out the door,* but Molly sipped her wine — one o'clock on a Saturday, third glass on the back deck — and dismissively waved an arm at me. *Isabella's married,* she said, *and a good Catholic,* adding that all the *best ones* come from Latin America. Beth looked at Farah, her nanny, who was with me and the children farther off in the yard; as though we weren't even there she said, *Or those Muslim countries, where she wouldn't dare.*

Farah and I know it's best to pretend we don't speak English well, to pretend there aren't American or British schools in Guatemala or Egypt that gave us fortunates the chance to leave for somewhere like here — to leave, but not to get good work. Farah's hung on for five years without crushing Beth, and I've spent more than three enduring Molly's daily reminders about what to feed Gemma. I know. I'm a better mother to her than I am to Gabriela. I'm better than Molly is for Trevor, too. He swears that he loves me and that he's leaving her, and he's always asking, *What will we do about your husband?*, relaxing again when I promise I'll take care of it, as soon as he wants me to. The only thing is, he says, he can't leave yet, because Gemma is too young to have just one parent.

But so is Gabriela.

# The Locked Out

*T*here were two locks: bolt and latch. From the street he turned his key, clunking the bolt, but when he pulled the door it didn't open. It was nine o'clock Saturday morning, and his girlfriend slept heavily inside the apartment above the shop. Her shift at the hospital had ended at 4:00 AM when he, finished work for the week, had been asleep at a friend's house after a few beers. It had begun raining around midnight and as neither he nor the friend owned an umbrella, he'd chosen the couch instead of walking home, texting her saying he would return in the morning. When she had entered, tired and presumably drenched, she must have thought nothing of sliding the latch across.

A call would wake her most gently, so he dialled, but her voicemail answered before any rings — her phone was off, or silenced. He texted and then he sent a short email, hoping one or the other would trigger a different sound. When neither elicited a response he sipped coffee from his paper cup and frowned. The rain was still falling, and the wind had picked up. His wet T-shirt clung to him and his feet squished in his sneakers' decaying soles.

Knocking would make next to no noise, as the door was a metal-framed piece of frequently graffitied frosted glass. Tapping it with a key or a coin was louder, and he tried it but still she didn't come downstairs. The push-button buzzer never had worked, and when he needed in, his habit was to pull and push the handle rapidly so that the door banged on the jamb. But the thundering would be hell to awake to, especially after working so late.

He heard a click and looked down to where the cat's silhouette put two clawed paws on the glass and stretched before it sat down. *A dog would bark*, he thought. He exhaled and gripped the handle and bang-bang-banged and waited. Nothing. He looked down at the animal's vague outline and tried to commune with it: *Go get her*, he willed, and then lowered himself into a squat and said, "Go get her," which drew a strange look from the shop owner who had come out to investigate. "You can sit in my store," the owner said, but he declined, saying, "She'll just be a minute. I'll try again." The shop owner smiled and returned to his counter, his door chime jingling behind him.

A car hissed on the wet street as it passed, masking his exhalation as he shook the door and tried to make enough noise without sounding desperate, or violent, or drunk — which he wasn't, and hadn't been the night before. But soaked anyway now, he thought maybe he should have gotten soaked last night, the way she must have on her walk home. His text to say he was staying out might have dashed her dream of peeling off their wet clothes with teeth chattering and stepping into a hot shower, both of them up too late but together, then crawling into bed like they had in university after too-loud music and shawarma when the bars closed.

Wasn't it possible that she had latched the door on purpose?

He began walking down the street, composing another text: *At the library, call me when you wake up.* From the shelf he chose a dog-eared copy of *The Lottery* and sat at a central table reading its first story, "The Intoxicated." He looked repeatedly at the phone, set to silent, and waited for its little red light to blink.

He wondered when the rain would stop.

# A Real Princess

Lauren had a Princess Mariella infant sleeper, a Princess Mariella high chair, baby bottle, sippy cup, Pull-Ups, sneakers, and now, a knapsack. The Princess Mariella Sheet and Canopy Set adorned her four-poster bed, and Princess Mariella's Fairy Magic Play House filled a corner of her room. Before school, she watched her Princess Mariella cartoons on video as she ate her Princess Mariella Cherry Yogurt with its collector spoon and, during free play in her kindergarten class, she always chose the Princess Mariella Colouring Book, which was just like the one she had at home. She coloured Mariella the same way every time: pink dress, purple puffy shoulders, yellow hair, and pretty blue eyes, like her own. When she came home from school, she turned on the TV and watched Princess Mariella, who climbed onto Prince Gulliver's white horse at the end of every episode and cooed, "I'm a real princess now, and so are you," which Lauren said along with her before sitting down to dinner, the Microwaveable Princess Mariella Chicken Fingers and Fries.

Lauren finished boarding school and grew into a woman and, after leaving the best women-only university with a failing grade midway through first semester, took a job at a video store on the ground floor of a major bank's skyscraper, where she rented out

# A Real Princess

DVD copies of *Princess Mariella: The Movie*, the new, live-action reboot advertised on every billboard in the city. At midnight, when her shift ended, she would change out of her uniform and into a dress in the store washroom and walk to Mariella, a restobar nearby that had recently paid a settlement in a copyright infringement case. The inside was decorated pink and purple and filled with women who, like Lauren, had dyed their hair so blonde that no one would mistake it for natural. Here she met her best friends, who spent the night luring lonely bean-counters into buying them one martini after another. At last call, one by one, her friends got into the bankers' sports cars and rode off, leaving Lauren behind. She always declined a ride from whichever man they'd left her and walked instead to the metro station. Never had they left behind her Gulliver.

One morning after yet another such night, Lauren awoke around eleven and made her way to work. In the train she put on makeup to cover the bags under her eyes. She shuffled into the store ten minutes late and planted herself behind the counter, opening the *Princess Mariella Double Digest*, an indulgent and regressive variety store purchase. She barely moved the rest of the day, intermittently reading and looking out the window until the bustle of rush hour filled the streets. The din was softer than usual, and new sounds mingled therein — clip-clops and whinnies and neighs. Past the front window rode a man in a black business suit, astride a white horse.

"Gulliver!" Lauren cried. She ran through the front door and onto the sidewalk, where she froze in place. In both directions, as far down the street as she could see, were clusters of men on white horses in their suits and their shiny black shoes. Lauren breathed in and waded into the slow traffic, looking for Gulliver. The first one to pass had to be The One, but which one was he? The horses streamed by. Lost in the white sea, she edged between them and plopped down on her bottom on the sidewalk. A tear ran down her face. One of the horses slowed.

"Pretty cool horse I got, huh?" said the man on top.

Lauren looked up. The man was square-jawed, his black hair neatly gelled, and his finely tailored suit had to be designer. He flashed a slick smile and asked, "Want to take a ride?"

Lauren smiled back and began to ask his name but stopped when she noticed, over his shoulder, a new billboard that had sprung up beside her skyscraper. It showed a new, limited-edition model of this year's white horse. Any of the men could be Gulliver for the right price. Lauren put her head in her hands and began to sob.

The man sneered at her and nudged his horse's side with his foot.

"Let's go," he muttered to the animal. "This one's a real princess."

## 99 Per Cent

*T*he Electra Glide stops, all black with batwing and hard bags. The portly rider in black leather steps off and looks into Christie Pits, removing his helmet to reveal a stars-and-stripes bandana. His face is sunburned pink and sports a long thick white goatee. He squints in the morning sun then turns his back to me. The gold-on-black bottom rocker reads "CANADA" but I can't make out the top one or what's in the centre of the patch, looking up only occasionally from the novel I'm reading at a picnic table under a tree, not wanting to stare — a Hells puppet club out east uses a similar colour scheme. What or who is he waiting for? Of course I think drug deal. They happen all the time on the park lip, but the characters are usually baggy-clothed and young, very young, with cockeyed baseball hats and neck tattoos.

It's a Sunday. This is heavy for a Sunday.

The biker crosses Christie Street's treed island and brick surface. He enters the Tim Hortons and I eye his ride a while. There's something less tough about a motorcycle with a trunk, but where else would he carry what he came to sell? A backpack would hide his colours — the colours he'd best be flying on club business — but then again, business seems to be the paper-wrapped

23

breakfast sandwich he's stuffing through his facial hair as he returns to the park.

He turns his head and so do I when a rumble comes down Bloor and a leaner Softail turns off urgently. Its obese rider wears a neutral expression under a thin mustache, blue shades, and orange half helmet; the skid lid matches the paint flames on his fuel tank and fenders. He's obviously late, guiding the bike to a reckless stop, and with his back to me he climbs off and hangs his helmet on his handlebars, revealing a bald spot on the back of his skull. He pulls his leather vest over his blue T-shirt and the men set off on foot, past tall trees toward the houses north of here to do God-knows-what.

They're still gone when next I look up, and in their place a boy of eight has stopped his teal bicycle. Beside the Harleys he balances with his toes on the ground, wearing a yellow T-shirt and black-and-red shorts. His brown hair needs cutting and curls out the back of a silver helmet. The hogs' front tires block his back one from view, which makes him look like an extension: a third wheel, a future. The kid's mother snaps a photo. I worry the men will return and demand her camera to destroy it, maybe toss her on one bike's back and roar away. I've seen *Sons of Anarchy*. But the next time I look up, the machines are alone again.

It's been an hour. I mark my page and leave the park. In my apartment I spend sixty more minutes on Google, scanning M.C. sites whose links are purple from the last time I visited. But today I find a new one, a Canada-only club; the patch looks pretty similar. Membership is restricted to military and police veterans, and the jackets are the toughest thing about them.

That's probably who the men were.

Probably.

# Every Night Is Like This

*D*o not forget Roberta, sixty-one, who held up a hand to you at the Dufferin and St. Clair streetcar stop and said "You're handsome," and "You couldn't be more than twenty-five," which made you blush and say, "I'm thirty-one," seeming to invite her to tell you something about herself, Roberta with the Coke-bottle glasses and the stringy, curled white hair who made you pinky-swear not to tell *anyone* before she told you her name (followed immediately by her age, her address, and the story of why she was finally leaving her apartment, and how it wasn't her fault her landlords were mad at her, it was their own fault they were mad at her, because she was a nice woman but just spent all the money she had on substances — corrected herself — supplies, which gave you a better sense of why the pinky was like a claw and why yours still hurt when you got home), because she needed someone to help her, take her arm first and then her walker and get her into the streetcar, which you did just as the rainstorm began and the driver greeted her by name, talking to her all the way to her stop while she alternated between laughing and screaming and crying, and the driver — you should never forget her either, because for both of them, every night is like this.

# Eclipse

*I*n Cathedral Square, the bells seem set on repeat, but the pattern is inconsistent. Chaotic. The tower stands separate from the church and flares out at the base — a skirt on the white cylinder in the pointy black hat — and a small staircase leads to an arched door, open, where you imagine ten children inside and an attendant saying, "Pull these ropes till you're tired," in Lithuanian, of course.

The sun is brilliant on the smooth granite stones. Across the square, stiff flags atop roofs snap, and though you think you can hear them, you can't because of the bells, steady and oppressive like silence or "Speak to Me", track one, *Dark Side of the Moon*. Your knees waver near the Gediminas statue and you rest against the pagan king, awaiting the terrified scream. You expect it to come from your own mouth.

The statue casts a long shadow on the white church. Preteens jump skateboards in slow motion, and families on Sunday walks become worker bees, small, swarming the hive. Atop the tower, the clock says five to five. No occasion, but the bells blare on.

Time.

You watch the belfry as you cross the square, your path a challenge to the clappers swinging back and forth, metronomes of disorientation. You reach the other side and Šventaragio Street,

# Eclipse

where the grand boulevard Gedimino dead-ends in a T. The light turns green, and when you advance the bells stop. Cars honk, and bicycles ring. People speak a language you don't. But traversing Šventaragio, you hear nothing.

The tower sounds two final *dongs* as you step from street to sidewalk. The din of the city filters back into your ears, and you feel more alone than ever.

# Camaleón de Santiago

Y ou stop ascending the stairs of Cerro Santa Lucía when you see a small lizard on the banister. It doesn't dare move and neither do you. Its head and forelegs are green as the tree it descended from, its middle is blue like the sky, and slowly its tail is greying from the tip to match the stone beneath it. You're just above the three-arched, goldenrod-coloured fountain that rises from the palms and sends five jets shooting down twice your height from a bronze Neptune into a pool on the marble-floored landing. You stare as the lizard keeps changing colour; it stares back, more afraid of you than you of it. You ask yourself, *Is it poisonous? What's it going to do next?* You hear the fountain and farther down on the big street you came from, the Alameda, buses shudder and hiss, motorcycles roar, construction machines boom in the excavation where Universidad Católica is expanding. Between you and the lizard, though, silence. Almost completely grey now, the reptile still hasn't moved and might still believe you haven't seen it, that you'll keep climbing undistracted to Darwin's Garden — 1827, he was here — and the narrow deck of Mirabel Tower, where you'll photograph the view: endless apartment buildings in all directions, the Andes in the distance still under huge snowcaps though it's summer here. You'll get home and see on Google Images that there are literally millions of photos just

# Camaleòn de Santiago

like yours. You'll also learn that chameleons don't even live in South America, and that your lizard is likely an anolis, which isn't native either — thousands are exported every year to pet stores all over the world, including those on the Alameda, whose proper name is Avenida Libertador General Bernardo O'Higgins, after the chief changeling hero in a city full of them — Juan Mackenna, Enrique Mac Iver — and what you are staring down is almost certainly a child's escaped pet: 27,000 Chilean pesos wasted, adapting before your eyes.

# Nate

*J* had texted from the night bus, 3:00 AM after we met, and late the next afternoon she had replied with obsessive requests for my photo. She was younger — kind of *a lot* younger — and didn't take well to my refusal, my *Haha you don't know who this is.*

I hadn't heard from her in the few months since, but I hadn't deleted her number, either. And then, while I was home watching a *Big Bang Theory* rerun, dripping in the late summer heat in just a pair of shorts, *Cindy* appeared backlit in blue on the vibrating Galaxy.

I didn't have to answer, but I did.

"Nate?"

I recognized the little whine in her voice.

*Who the hell is Nate?* I thought. *She's got the wrong number.*

"Yeah, it's me," I said.

———

Betting she'd be too fucked up to realize I wasn't Nate was bad, but being right was worse. From her dumpy lobby I texted *Here* — buzzers never work in these places — and through the glass door I watched her teeter down the stairs. She led with shoeless, black-stockinged feet, then firm legs under a short black

Name

dress, its scooped neck bagging over breasts smaller than the designer had imagined. Mascara had run down her cheeks, her dyed-blonde hair was tousled; I thought it might be a new style but it looked too authentic. She opened the door and wrapped me in her arms, burying her head in my chest, sobbing. The sound was awful, but not as bad as the puke-stink from her mouth.

*What have I gotten into?*

I closed my arms around her. We shared a still moment till she wobbled onto tiptoes to kiss me. I turned my head and took the barf-lips on the cheek. She slurred, "I'm so glad you came," and looked up with absent, wide, green eyes. They were pretty; *she* was pretty.

Neutrally as I could, I said, "Of course."

Running a hand slowly down my chest, she asked, "We gonna do this here?" then pulled back, laughing. She took my hand and wrapped my forearm tightly in hers to lead me up the dirty stairs. As we walked the dingy brown carpet in the dim hall I kept thinking, *Nate. Your name is Nate.*

It should have been easy to remember. I was sure I was in her phone as Nate because I met her at Nate's, this crumbling bar I'd been drunk in dozens of times, beginning years ago but not so much lately, not since hipster kids like Cindy had taken it over. She hadn't been this dressed up the first time we met, but wearing something that fit right in: a skirt and blouse, I think, dark green below tawny, maybe. I could have asked if she still had the outfit, to jog her memory, but it wouldn't have helped. She had been just as fucked up then.

—

31

# HAMBURGER

Her apartment smelled musty and various smokes lingered in the air. In the kitchen dirty dishes climbed out of the sink and occupied the counter. Laundry was piled high in a living room corner. In front of the couch she gave me a light push to sit me down. She lowered herself beside me and clumsily took my cheeks in her hands. She looked me over a moment. If she was looking for someone actually named Nate, she'd figure it out now.

She stared into my eyes forever, a hammered astronomer methodically aiming her telescope quadrant by quadrant. In my head I was already working out how to spin this epic strikeout back to the guys on my hockey team, how to get in the most possible suspense and titillation. But a smile came over her face, maybe a genuine one, and she removed the hands to reach for a pipe on the coffee table beside an ashtray full of roaches. She lit the pipe and sucked deeply then offered it to me. It had been years since I had smoked pot — at least I thought this was pot. I took it and inhaled a plastic taste before I coughed. She turned the wide greens on me and they looked disappointed.

"I'll be right back," she said, getting up and walking to the bathroom. I could only imagine how dirty it was. Through the closed door I heard her say, "God, I look horrible," then the running water, then her peeing and flushing and opening the cabinet; the water again. As I waited I thought about it: should I ask why she'd been crying? Did I care? What if I didn't?

When she came back she had taken off the stockings and had cleaned the black streaks off her face. She straddled my lap and kissed my mouth. She tasted like mouthwash now.

—

# Nate

In her bed we did everything before I finally came, exhausted and sweaty and even kind of in pain. I hadn't realized how badly I needed to get laid. She fell asleep right afterward and started to snore, splayed on her back, small tits spilling barely over the top of her ribcage. The night-table lamp was still on. I stared at the ceiling and thought about how few words I had used tonight: there'd been maybe twenty, and some repeated, particularly *yeah* and *Cindy* and *oh*. I wondered how this girl — woman, twenty-three, she had told me — had decided I was the one to make her forget the thing she wasn't talking about, the thing I wasn't asking after.

Of course, I wasn't the one. Nate was. Whoever Nate was. Whoever *was* Nate, I should say — there might have been a few. I thought back to how we had met. There wasn't much there. We hadn't talked much. She *couldn't* talk much. She'd been slurring then, too. In short, we had downed shots and shared smokes on the bar's back patio until the server cut us off. She hadn't known enough to go home, and neither had I. The buddy I had come with had taken off hours before, laughing when I said I was going to see if I'd get anywhere with the blonde — who at the time was picking her cigarette up off the ground and putting it back into her mouth.

I felt now like I had taken advantage. But we *had* traded texts, we had clearly kept each other's numbers, and tonight, she had called me — or Nate, at least.

I got up from the bed and held the condom on, pulling it off in front of the toilet, then flushing it. The bathroom faucet was speckled with toothbrushing spit and dirt was visible on the floor tiles. On the vanity, hair product bottles had accumulated, some with crusted liquid worming out their caps. I squinted through the built-up spatter on the mirror and looked at my naked self, down to my belly button, as far as the tiny glass showed, then up again to my face. I had to turn away from the beginnings of the smug smile, the one that follows me into the dressing room when I've got another yarn for the boys.

——

I gathered up my clothes, putting on my tee and jeans without waking her. I was to the door and almost gone, crouched with one sandal on when she appeared from the bedroom. A man's long dress shirt, half-buttoned, covered most of her. She blinked the big greens and hit me with the whine again.

"Like it?"

She gestured to her torso, brushing her chest with her fingers as she did.

"Yeah," I said, "It's hot," adding no new words to the count.

"Of course you do," she said. "It's yours."

I studied the pale blue stripes on the white shirt. It was possible. I'd owned a few like this, bought practically in bulk for my office job. But the first time I'd met Cindy, hadn't I left the bar alone? Or was I confusing it with some other night I had waited for the late bus? And I wouldn't have come home in my under-shirt, would I? Would Nate?

I strapped on my second sandal and stood up.

"Keep it," I said with a shrug. "I gotta go."

In exaggerated protest, she stuck out her bottom lip, but then she retracted it. The look in her eyes sharpened. She pushed a tired hand through her bangs and her voice flattened.

"What was your name again?"

"John."

# Nate

*Shit.*

*Nate.*

"You want to do this again sometime, John?" she asked.

"Maybe when I'm not like this?"

"Yeah, maybe," I said.

"'Kay," she said, yawning. "Call me."

"Yeah," I said again.

We held each other's eyes a few seconds before I reached for the knob. My head spun. It really had been ages since I'd gotten high, and whatever this was, it wasn't weed. Without looking back I pulled the door shut and headed for the bus stop — not the Blue Night, just the regular one. As I waited I keyed *Talk tomorrow* into our conversation and pressed send.

I felt dizzy and sick to my stomach.

I didn't want to be Nate in the morning.

# Pleasure Craft

*T*hey only insisted because Carrie had left me. They had replied-all with exclamation marks when I ran out of excuses. They lent me a sleeping bag and said, "It won't be the same without you, Karl." They refused to turn the car around when I said I'd forgotten my towel.

———

We had a great time! We just relaxed, played cards, sat around the fire drinking beer. We even had Karl up. We knew Carrie's reasons for dropping him and moving to New York — we learned them at the going-away party she hadn't told him about. We decided we should still invite him to the cottage, though. We kind of thought we had to. We didn't know if he had friends other than us.

———

They started on me about water-skiing the first night. They countered my "I don't swim well," "I'll break my ankles," and "I don't want to fall" with "You'll have a life jacket," "Your feet pop out of the skis," and "Dude — falling on water doesn't hurt."

———

We had rented the boat for nine o'clock. We passed Karl on our way to the marina. We weren't sure after last night that we should be driving, and there he was running, sweating through his shirt. We opened the window to offer a ride but he said he needed ten K today. We weren't going to talk him out of it.

———

They called to me, "We'll show you a few times," and "We'll get you used to the idea." They revved the rumbling old fish-and-ski into open water. They stayed in full view and took turns behind the boat. They didn't care that I wasn't watching.

———

We found Karl on the dock, face-down in a fat paperback. We thought of rich Brianne Beaufort from high school, who threw pool parties but was too embarrassed of her body to swim. We hadn't gone to high school with Karl, just Carrie, but he had to know the laws of nature. We never let Brianne sit dangling her legs in the water. We always threw her in.

———

They said the water was clean, and warm to boot. They heckled, "Get up!" and "Come on!" and they splashed me. They teased that I cradled my book like a running back with a football. They said, "You know we're not going to let up, Karl."

———

We showed him proper form on the dock, legs bent, arms straight-straight-straight. We said, "Anyone can do it," and when he started worrying — "I'm going to regret this," "I'm going to die," etc. — we took a lucky stab at his Achilles heel: we said it would be something to write about. We reminded him he had a life jacket. We said, "Get in the boat, Karl."

—

They moved aside, feet clanking stray paddles against the floor, and they slow-clapped when I got in. They opened up the motor. They yelled over the engine about wind and spray, and they exalted that though families ringed the shore — grilling hot dogs, playing tag, mowing lawns — the twenty-footer had the lake to itself. They stopped and threw the skis over the side, tow handle over the stern, rope trailing. They looked at me, all of them together.

—

We waited a long time for Karl to jump. We wondered how long he'd stand there and stare into the water. We were relieved to see the fear in his face settle. We breathed out when he splashed in. We didn't need to hear him complain about the cold.

—

They must have been bored. They must have laughed at the skis insistently floating up, the black rubber footholds sliding off me time and again as I'd get one on then twist and flop to retrieve the other. They wouldn't have heard the sucking sound when my feet were finally in; they got only a tentative thumbs-up. They hit the throttle, pulled the rope taut, and snatched me up from the water.

—

We got our phones ready to film. We held our breath while his skis hopped. We watched his legs straighten — too straight! We winced at one another when he Supermanned into an explosion of water. We said, "Man, his skis launched like missiles!"

—

They laughed, of course — who wouldn't? — but apologized when they brought back the tow rope. They had told me how to get up. They hadn't told me what to do next. They claimed no one stands the first time. They said I should try again, just let the boat do the work — "And Karl, for God's sake, keep your legs bent."

—

We knew after three falls he was sick of it. We heard him curse after each crash and understood what Carrie had said: so hard on himself. We said the last one wasn't his fault. We had hit the throttle too hard. We said, "One more, you have to do one more."

—

They all paused after I shook my head, both arms over the gunwales to support myself, asking, "How many more times do you need to see me fail?" They said with a little disappointment, "Actually, we want you to succeed."

—

I keep my weight back and let my ankles unlock. I come up gently, holding my arms straight. I keep my knees bent. I stabilize. I skim the surface. I hear the whooping from the boat; I add my own high-pitched cry from deep in my chest. I yell till I run out of breath, and I just ride after that, allowing the outboard to become a faint hum in the distance. I have nothing in my mind — no them, no us, no Carrie, *nothing* — and finally I think, "I might be happy."

I feel a ski slide out from under me.

# US 101

*T*he driver. One passenger riding shotgun. Fifteen more seats, mostly filled. The white shuttle rattles in the high-occupancy lane and some of us look out the windows, tall windows, at the drought-browned hills outside San Jose as I settle in for the two-hour trip to Carmel. It's near dusk, the blue sky's marbled with white clouds, and the jovial forty-something black driver and the white sixty-plus seeming veteran beside him are comparing notes on the fishing around Monterey, an entry point to a whole-ride conversation, which I recognize because I've already had two today, with a songwriter on the flight from Toronto to LAX and with a sculptor on the San Jose leg. Traffic's already made us half an hour late and the driver's wife has already called, setting off a cheery digitized song. He's not the only one on a cell, not by a long shot — nearly everyone has tunes in earphones, or a movie on a tablet, and faintly there's music trickling all the way to the back bench of five seats where, in the middle one, I'm scribbling in a notebook. Minutes ago even I was staring at my phone, cursing the stone-age BlackBerry I refuse to upgrade but thankful for the bus' Wi-Fi. I mean, Robin Williams died yesterday and now so has Lauren Bacall, which makes it almost irrelevant that I've squeezed seventeen hours of daylight out of today thanks to the time difference, or that we're slowly wending our way into a beautiful California sunset, Burger Kings and Quality Inns and Targets along the freeway be damned. There is beauty here, in the compounds of car dealerships and the backs of SUVs jockeying lanes as they pass, beauty at sixty-five radar-enforced miles per hour and in the frustration of being late and in the way the driver tells his wife it should only be an hour, just over an hour, and goes on to talk of making good time with the vet — look at that hair, slicked and short and so thin and white now. He must be a vet.

Beauty's in the elderly Japanese couple in front of me, too, talking in soft language the rest of us don't understand as they enjoy the hills beyond the tinted windows, hills my camera can't capture, beauty that trickles through despite the salty snacks and bottled water and phone full of music I've piled on the seat beside mine, despite the notebook and the pen and the *bing* of someone's text message as we pass through a small forest big enough to deprive me of the light I need. The road narrows to two lanes from the five that left San Jose and we're passing Hollister — it's a town, not just a T-shirt — and one more person gets a phone call as the highway gets so bumpy I can't write clearly. There is roadwork. There are orchards and horse paddocks and a sudden, massive storm cloud and feelings that all this mediation, that tinny beat from somewhere up front and the urge to write anything at all are in the way. I will not put in my earbuds. I will not. I will not check my Facebook, or return that email, or even keep writing. There are *Cheap Cars* and *Your Pet's Best Friend* near the exit to Prunedale and the first garish black-and-green sign pointing the way to Cannery Row. There is a short stop and a slammed door, an idling engine then a turnabout that puts us back on the highway. An astonished mutter from the driver as he mistakes himself for on time, then laughs it off with an "Oh well" as we remaining passengers laugh with him. Trees block the sunset when I want to take a crappy point-and-shoot, grainy from the glass and blurry, seatbacks and someone's nose in the shot. And then we round a curve. The red sun appears, wedged between distant slopes; a charcoal ceiling thickens, rising like a hill just born. I snap the photo. It looks terrible. There is beauty here.

*medium*

# The Short Life of Gary Q. Stuffholder III

*T*able Nineteen is at the back of the reception hall, near the DJ booth and bar where all night we'll overhear slurring requests for bad songs and watery cocktails through the speeches, all of them, eight a side for bride and groom, enough for guys-against-girls baseball. I was first through the dining room doors after champagne in the lobby, and by setting down my purse I staked out the farthest possible seat from the podiums, back to the wall, with a clear view for when the bride's mascara starts running.

Sarah's my best friend, but I've always known I'm not hers. In a past life we were shooter girls together, but she's a pretty blonde who took public relations in college, working weekends just for extra money; for me, the job was it, killing time till I decided what to study. She graduated the spring before I started my accounting certificate, and a downtown firm hired her right away. Brett swept her off her feet soon after. They've already bought a house and dog and done their engagement photos on the front porch. They're all over her Facebook, and there are prints on every table, the smiles almost too big and the Labradoodle Gertrude's tongue hanging out moronically. If that makes me sound jealous, well fine. I am. Rob and I have lived together almost two years, but when the invite came it said *Emily Waters and guest.*

# The Short Life of Gary Q. Stuffholder III

Most years, wedding season would be over by now, but Sarah wanted it this late because she had already stood up at four — *four* — ceremonies this summer, meaning four engagement parties, four showers, four bachelorettes, and four weddings, the last in San Francisco, where *her* best friend Katie lives now. In my minute with Sarah in the receiving line she said she was so glad her day had *finally* come, that this summer had *just been so crazy*, and that she couldn't believe she hadn't seen me in *so* long but was *so* glad I came. She looked around and beside me and then she asked, "Where's Rob?" Before I could answer she put her hand on my shoulder. "Oh, Em," she said. "Don't tell me." I nodded. "Well, maybe he wasn't the right one for you, hon — but don't worry, you'll meet him someday." She smiled and winked. "Maybe even tonight. You know, Brett's brought a lot of his friends from the law office, and . . . "

I quit listening. Rob and I didn't break up. It's the last weekend of October and he's dug in again. Every year, he and his idiot baseball team camp out in one player's house and watch the World Series, getting smashed and making that player's WAG's life hell. It can last ten days if it goes to Game Seven, and it has this year. Tonight's the finale. Too pissed off to ask him, I used a wire coat hanger to zip up my new black dress while Rob wasted the afternoon on the couch, flipping through the sports channels in his Cardinals jersey and backwards cap as though I might forget he had other plans tonight. He's never been to St. Louis. I have no idea why he cheers for that team and I'm pretty sure I don't care.

DavidandSylvia join me first at the table. David articled at the same firm as Brett, and Sylvia's his wife. They're both originally from New York and they go on for a few minutes about how *amazing* it is that they had to come *all the way to Toronto* before they met. David asks, "Rye and ginger?" and Sylvia smiles and nods. He walks to the bar and by the time he's back, Sylvia and I are shaking hands with LeighandChuck. Leigh, the receptionist in Sarah's office, wears a navy pantsuit and is easily fifty — "Mother Hen," she says. She laughs at her own joke. I vaguely remember Sarah using the nickname. Her husband Chuck talks in grunts and may have no job aside from eating. When David returns he mumbles something about whether the Cards will take it and Leigh shoots Chuck a steely look before he can answer: *I told you. No baseball.* I excuse myself and head for the bar, wondering if that's how Rob and I will talk one day. It seems more efficient than actually talking. I return with a gin and tonic and meet our table's last couple, GregandSam. Sam grew up in the house next door to Brett and played trucks with him, he says. "Until Sam switched to Barbies," Greg interjects, and the two of them laugh while Chuck gives them cut-eye.

It's happened again. I'm at the Randoms Table.

The chairs fill, except for one directly across from me, its back to the double head tables. At each place setting there's a cardboard box the size of a coffee cup, though I know Sarah chose better favours. I can picture Chuck still drinking out of his and Leigh's wedding mugs, and the flat of spares he keeps in the basement in case of breakage. Sylvia unties the purple ribbon on her box and says, "Candle," nonchalantly setting it beside her on the empty chair. "Oh," she says. "Sorry — is anyone sitting here?" All six look at me and I shrug. "Unless someone else is here alone." Leigh looks truly sad. Greg snorts. "One of Brett's ex-girlfriends?" I'm the last to start laughing. DavidandSylvia quieten first. They look at me caringly. "No," I protest, "I'm *Sarah's* friend," and I force another laugh. I'm alone on this one. Sam rescues me by leaning in with a wine bottle. "Who wants red?" he asks. Chuck shakes his shaved balding head and points to his beer. I say, "I'll have some," and remove the napkin from my wine glass, one of three glasses for me, including the G-and-T and the water. I also have a bread plate, a regular plate, and three forks and two spoons and the favour; multiply by eight and add two bottles of red and white, and water (sparkling *and* still), and the table gets crowded. Chuck taps his temple and his grey mustache ripples. "Good idea, Sylvia," he says, leaning a bit to hand her his box. Sam sets the bottle down and hands his box to Greg. Greg hands two to Leigh, who relays three to David, who passes them to Sylvia one by one. She stacks them on the chair. Sylvia puts her hand out to take mine, but I say, "It's all right, I'll just put it in my purse." She eyes my black clutch and says, "Are you kidding?" I laugh and say, "Right." I hand it across and she adds it to the pile. Leigh pours herself some white. "Everyone have a glass?" she asks. "Everyone but Gary," Greg says. Sam raises an eyebrow. "Gary?" Greg says, "Yeah, Gary," and points at the box pile: three rows of two and my single one a head, like a Lego man. A slow laugh builds in Chuck until it's tumbling out of him in heavy *Ha-ha-ha*s. "Gary," he says, wiping a tear from one eye. "Gary! A toast to Gary!" David looks around the table. He raises his glass and clears his throat. "I can already tell this will be a great time," he says, which makes me think he has a future at an embassy. "To new friends." We reach in to clink glasses but before we can, Chuck roars, "And to the best of them — Gary the Stuffholder!" Everyone laughs, even me, and we all push our glasses together and take a drink. Greg looks at Chuck and says slyly, "Gary Q. Stuffholder . . . the third." The table erupts again. I stop laughing first.

# HAMBURGER

—

Throughout the speeches, staggered between courses, I watch the head tables and the podiums beside them and let the Gary chair — Rob's chair — blur out of focus. There's plenty of spoon-on-glass racket after each speaker, or group: his friends from home, her friends from home; his friends from school, her friends from school; his parents, her parents, and — *finally* — the happy couple. I'm watching our vacant setting, where the plate hasn't been replaced since the appetizer, which Chuck ate after his own, crumpling the extra napkin and telling the caterers, "I don't know, I think Gary just went to the restroom," angling for a bonus steak, no doubt. We've been piling our bread plates and used cocktail glasses and wine and water bottles in front of the Gary chair and Chuck's hooted, "Bang-up job!" with every dish sent down, or "My God, Gary, you're a tank — *another* beer?" with each empty. I wasn't the only one waiting for Sarah and Brett to finish their thank-yous, and cry, "Let's party!" The guests took to the dance floor like an Elvis movie in slow-motion. My table-mates rushed to the cluster at the bar. I stayed put and now I'm slowly sipping my espresso, looking at full families slow-dancing, from Grandma and Grandpa Somebody still holding each other fifty years later to the twin four-year-old girls in matching purple dresses twirling from each of Daddy's arms, whoever Daddy is. Sure as hell won't be Rob. I scan the room and realize: Sarah is the only person I know here. Before today, I only met Brett once, at the engagement party. I empty the small cup and pick up my purse and snatch off Gary's head before I leave the table. Someone's drawn a smiley face on the box in blue pen. From the lobby I call a cab. The twenty minutes it will take are plenty to get my coat. Use the ladies' room. On my way out I swing the door open and it almost hits Sarah. Her eyes widen and her mouth droops a bit, in that over-dramatic sadness the bride has to show when you leave. "Are you going home already?" I swoop in to hug. "It was lovely," I say. "The food was so good and my table was — " She breaks the embrace, cutting me off, and mock-slaps me on the shoulder. "I heard," she says, eyes lighting up. "Is *that* where you're going now?" Her smile grows. "Where?" I ask. "You know." Sarah laughs. "Come *on*," she says. I look at her blankly. "*Gary*," she says in an exaggerated whisper, grabbing my arm. "DavidandSylvia said you totally hit off with this guy, Gary! Who is he? One of Brett's parents' friends' sons, or something? I don't even remember inviting him."

I pull away, muttering, "Gary is so dead when I get home," and I turn on my heel.

# Osvaldo's Guitar

*P*edro lives under a thatched palm roof with seven chickens, off a clay road where his father Juan's bicycle trails red-brown clouds every morning when he leaves to pick plantains. The house's wall-less wooden joists stand in concrete left over from the new school in Manzanilla. Pedro learns to spell *gracias* on the first day, and by the end of his first year he knows enough English to write a card to Señor Russ Watkins and his wife Judy in Woodside, Oklahoma. It's not on the globe, but Señor Patterson says that in Woodside everyone has a car, and so much to eat every day that they can send food, and clothes, and money to places like Manzanilla to help families like Pedro's buy school uniforms for their children.

Señor Patterson only teaches English. Esmerelda Martínez, who went to university in Managua, teaches everything else in Spanish. Her daughter Alejandra is ten, like Pedro, and before Señor Patterson and the orange *camiones* arrived, she and Pedro spent their days chasing each other through the trees, stopping only when they reached the fence surrounding the Gringo resort.

Every Semana Santa, Alejandra asks Pedro to come with her, to dance at the *fiesta* and to eat all the *gallo pinto* he wants. But as his family has nothing to bring, his parents forbid him to go. Spring after spring, when Pedro tells this to Alejandra, she smiles and says, "Maybe next year."

—

Manuel's house is made of cinder blocks covered in smoothed mortar and painted bright blue. It stands tall on the roadside, the trees around it cut down long ago, and its windows have bars, and screens, and glass that can be opened. Before the school was built, Manuel stayed inside every day, eating chili-flavoured Zambos chips and watching American TV on satellite.

Manuel's father Berto is a police officer. In the morning he gets into the *camión* with the blue and white flag sticker on its tailgate and follows the cement-brick road to the highway. By *almuerzo* he's back from Chinandega with his orders, checking papers and taking forty *córdoba* where the bricks meet the dirt track to Manzanilla.

When Berto stops Pedro's father's bicycle, Juan looks down at his feet and reaches into the handlebar basket. He offers the policeman two plantains and hopes Berto won't choose today to use the automatic rifle slung over his back.

Before the school was built, Pedro sometimes worked with his father. When they met Berto, the boy hung his head, afraid to see his reflection in the state-issued sunglasses.

—

Señor Patterson is nothing like the Sunday School teachers. He reads books to the children and wears costumes, and some afternoons he invites the Gringos to the school. The American men load the boys into the back of their *camión* and take them to the baseball diamond, which doubles as a cow pasture. The women walk the girls to their neighbour Osvaldo's, where they mount ponies and ride to the beach. Señor Patterson sings and plays guitar, too, crashing the strings to make chords. His songs are about adding and subtracting numbers, and how to say *por favor* and *gracias* in America. One day Osvaldo walks to the school and invites himself in. "*Guitarra, por favor,*" he says. He grins when Señor Patterson relinquishes it.

Osvaldo plucks the strings slowly, and softly. The children recognize his songs and clamour to sing the loudest.

From then on, when the Gringos come, Osvaldo comes too. The boys who don't play baseball and the girls scared of ponies sit cross-legged on the concrete floor and listen to the neighbour, who now brings his own guitar. Unlike Señor Patterson's, which is black with copper-wound wires, Osvaldo's has soft nylon strings and a warm wood-grain finish.

At first, half the children stay behind and await their turn to try. But as dry season carries on, baseball and ponies prove easier to master, and Osvaldo's students dwindle to two: Pedro and Manuel.

Osvaldo teaches the boys arpeggios, plucking the strings individually to make chords more delicate and fluid than Señor Patterson's. During his turn, Pedro easily mirrors Osvaldo, and when he finishes he passes the guitar to Manuel. Scrunching his face and jumping like a monkey, Manuel misses all the notes. Osvaldo and Pedro laugh until, eventually, Manuel moves his fingers down the neck to play an E, striking a series of defiant rumbles before giving the instrument back.

The last song in Osvaldo's lesson is always *De Colores*, and when he finishes, he leans his guitar in the corner at the front of the classroom, where it awaits the next special afternoon — or, as the school door doesn't lock, the next time either boy comes to practise.

Pedro goes straight home from school to feed the chickens. And every night, after finishing his rice and beans, he walks back. The matches his mother sends him to get from the *pulpería* rattle in his pocket, and when he arrives he draws one to light the candle on Señor Patterson's desk.

Manuel waits in front of the schoolhouse after class for Berto, who lurches the white *camión* up the road and then stops to lift his son into the cab. At home they eat the food Berto buys in the city and watch movies until Manuel's bedtime.

Alone, Pedro blisters his fingers, practising notes and scales again and again. He doesn't stop until he has only enough strength left to walk home.

———

A band is booked for the *fiesta* long before the glistening ribbons are hung over the town's dusty road. There's little belief the musicians will find tiny Manzanilla come Sunday, but the townspeople don't despair. News has spread about the schoolhouse prodigy; day or night, going to or coming from his practice, mothers and fathers greet Pedro, grinning and saying things like, "Maybe that band won't show up," and, "Maybe *you*'ll have to play."

Pedro knows he has to be ready. Thursday, after dinner, he returns to the school to practise once more before the weekend. The door groans as he opens it, and after a moment, the candle casts its familiar glow. Pedro feels for the guitar in the dusky corner, but instead finds only the cool cement wall.

—

Friday morning, Pedro awakes to shouting. Near the road, his father stares at the ground as Señor Patterson pleads with the policeman.

"Berto, *por favor*. We don't know that Pedro stole the guitar."

"His father is a plantain picker." He juts a finger at Juan. "They are the poorest family in town. Pedro wants to play this weekend, and he has no guitar. Who *else* might have taken it?"

Juan lifts his head and looks straight at Berto.

"Manuel."

The policeman removes his sunglasses, showing Juan the scowl behind them.

"Are you calling my son a thief?"

"You called my son the same."

"Lying peasant!" Berto grabs Juan by the shoulders and bellows, "*Where is the guitar?*"

Shrinking, Juan says, "You may look around, Señor. Please, you will see. It is not here."

Berto stamps to the fire pit and upsets a boiling pot, extinguishing the flames in a puff of ash. He turns next to the centre of the cement pad and flips the rickety table high into the air. The ceramic dishes land a few feet away and shatter.

"Stop, please!" Pedro's mother begs.

Berto breathes in harshly through his nose, and then he stalks back to his truck.

—

Later, after mass, Berto meets Juan at the end of the dirt road. The officer's automatic is already off his shoulder.

"One hundred *córdoba* today," he taunts. "It's a holiday."

"You know I have no money," Juan says. "But tonight, I will give — "

Berto brings the weapon to his hip. He points the barrel at Juan, who falls immediately to his knees.

"No, Berto, *por favor* — "

The butt of the rifle connects with Juan's jaw, and when he crumples, Berto applies it to his ribs and his back. He hefts Juan into the truck's box and drives the unconscious body to its home, where he rolls it off the bed.

"You peasants," Berto sneers. "It's your fault people don't trust each other."

———

Juan can no longer stop Pedro from attending the *fiesta*, this is certain. Pedro takes one look at him moaning in his hammock and goes to beg his mother's permission. She sighs and sends him to pick plantains. He nearly protests, but then she says, "If you gather enough for the fish soup — *for everyone* — then you can go."

Pedro works all day. He fills his basket ten times with twenty plantains and piles them in front of the house. His mother is left with no choice.

Before the vigil ends that night, Pedro has forgotten the guitar. He falls asleep smiling, and awakes the next morning the same way.

On the roadside, with his two hundred plantains, he waits for the Gringos to pass. He knows they'll stop and deliver him and his crop to the schoolhouse where the *fiesta* is held now, having moved from the much smaller Iglesia del Cristo last year.

A rumbling *camión* approaches but it's not from the resort. It's white. Pedro steps back from the road.

Berto leans out the window.

"Pedro! Would you like a ride?"

The boy shakes his head.

"How will you get the plantains to town without a truck, little man? Let me help you."

Stock still, Pedro watches Berto climb out. He walks to the basket and lifts it, emptying it into the box. Only when he kneels to fill it again does Pedro join him. When the plantains are all loaded Berto holds the door open.

"Come on, get in," he says, holding Pedro's arm as the boy jumps from the running board to the passenger seat.

Manuel is in the middle of the bench. Between them sits Osvaldo's guitar.

———

With the band nowhere to be found, Señor Patterson calls on Pedro. The boy comes running to the front of the classroom and takes his seat beside the teacher. Señor Patterson hands his own guitar to Pedro, and immediately the boy stretches for the tuning keys. His teacher has already adjusted them but, to be sure, Pedro plucks each string once.

The audience applauds, and then they go silent.

Pedro takes a breath but he doesn't begin playing.

"Manuel!" he yells.

His classmate emerges from the crowd, stone-faced and ready to be punished. In his arms he holds Osvaldo's guitar.

Pedro asks, "Did you practise?"

"*Sí.*" A hint of a smile waits at the corners of his mouth.

# Osvaldo's Guitar

Pedro motions to his right. Señor Patterson gives up his chair and Manuel sits down.

Slowly, Pedro plucks the first notes of *De Colores*. Manuel listens more than he plays, carefully watching Pedro's hands, and when he recognizes the E position, he sneaks in the only chord he knows.

Berto stands at the back of the audience in his navy slacks and cap, sunglasses clipped to his powder-blue police shirt. His automatic is locked in the *camión* outside, safely hidden under the seat. And at the front of the schoolhouse, Alejandra dances.

# Be Your Own Master

*D*r. Benny promised Mat that if he wasn't satisfied, if in a week he wasn't standing up to everyone who pushed him around — *used to* push him around — he could have a full refund minus shipping and handling. The promise wasn't to Mat specifically, but Dr. Benny's program had already helped hundreds of people; not *thousands*, not *millions*, but the infomercial hadn't been running long. Mat had only seen it during late-night soft-core on channel 57.

The people in the ad were smiley — too smiley, but wasn't this advertising? — save for one particular sad sack, balding and overweight and downcast. On the verge of tears he looked away from the camera and said, "My wife knocked me out three separate times, twice with a cast-iron pan. Without Dr. Benny's help I don't know how I could have left her." He was an actor, of course they were all actors, but it was this testimonial, not "I was a waitress and now I make six figures," that drew Mat's fingers to the phone.

His wife, Marnie, grumbled from the bedroom. "You'd better not be ordering things from TV." She worked twelve-hour days as a counsellor at the penitentiary outside the city and had gone to bed at nine.

Mat pretended not to hear her and lowered his voice as he confirmed his credit card details. In less than forty-eight hours, the life-changing, six-CD *Be Your Own Master* kit would be at his front door. He replaced the receiver in its cradle and turned off the TV. He stood up tall when he rose from the couch and made his way to the bedroom. These were the first steps. In a week, the world would meet a new Mat.

He didn't shower or brush his teeth before leaving the next morning, and his light hair, what was left of it, was almost flat atop his head. The alarm at five thirty had surprised him, as had each of the six snoozes, and he bolted out of the house into the still-dark morning and toward Main Street Coffee Co., where he had worked for two years since being downsized in 2010. His stride lagged in the snow today — his neighbours rarely shovelled their walks — and he pushed off harder on each step.

He dreaded this hustle every morning, and the way his manager, Kevin, would glance at the clock then mock-congratulate him for having finally consummated his marriage or, depending on his mood, wryly chide him about another night in front of channel 57 with his dick in his hand. This first half-hour, the block of honest time before the fake smile and the *coming right up* was plastered on for every customer, was the worst. It always wound up with Kevin reminding Mat that he'd done time — that those boys inside change your life in a hurry — and that Mat had best get hard or get jumping off a cliff. The pep talk would end and Kevin would morph his mouth into his lopsided grin and make his way to the front door, letting in the two or three people already lined up — always already lined up — and apologizing for the wait. The earliest customers would be the pickiest, too, bringing their lips to the rims of their paper cups and making small slurps before asking, "Is this *non*-fat?" Mat would assure them it was but Kevin would bust in anyway, superior and cool with his small black hoop earrings, saying, "Let's be sure — Mat, why don't you make another?"

Lost in the thought and sweating under his old ski jacket, Mat turned the corner onto Main Street. A bicycle whizzed by and a burly arm clipped his shoulder. His left ankle twisted; he grunted as he fell. Shifting on the ground and attempting to stand up, he focused on the few lighted bulbs across the street in the closed-down movie theatre's marquee. He rose slowly toward the sign but a large, rough hand pushed him down.

The prison had come to town in the fifties. The bike was one of the older tricks.

A man in a beat-up leather coat, head shaved, leaned over Mat. "Give me your money," he growled through broken teeth. "Hurry up."

"I," Mat stammered, "I don't have any."

The attacker reared back and drove his fist under Mat's eye. Mat yelped. "I swear! I don't!"

"Credit card," the man barked, cocking his arm again. "Cell phone. Watch."

"I — "

The robber punched again. Mat tasted blood. He said, "Okay," and reached into the back pocket of his black work slacks. "Just please don't hit me again." He handed over his wallet, from which the man took the Visa. He threw the wallet back at Mat's chest.

"Phone."

Mat shook his head.

"No phone."

A beefy hand shot out and grabbed Mat's throat.

"Don't lie."

Mat exhaled and reached into his slacks again, removing his iPhone. "It's old," he said, grimacing and looking away as he held it out, babbling as he awaited the next punch. "It's got the big charger, it'll be hard to sell — "

No impact came. Slowly Mat looked up; he saw only the marquee. The attacker had fled, and Mat still held the phone. He wiped a hand over his mouth and stood up, examining the shine on his black glove. He began limping down the street.

He was later than ever, but he had a good excuse, and when he entered, Kevin stared, mouth slightly open. Neither said a word as Mat hung his coat in the back room. He took the first-aid kit from the wall and headed to the restroom, where he cleaned the cut under his eye with peroxide and covered it with a Band-Aid. When he emerged he tied on his apron and set to work making fresh pots of all seven varieties of coffee. Kevin called out orders from the till as normal, but today he took Mat's side when customers questioned him.

Kevin's earrings were nothing compared to the scar on his cheek or the awful tattoos that peeked out of his rolled-up black sleeves. When asked about them, he would say, "I made some mistakes," or sometimes more bluntly, "I got them inside," and he countered the nervous expressions by adding, "But I couldn't stay out without Main Street Coffee Company. Their rehabilitation program is the best in the country." He would then offer to get a pamphlet from the storeroom. More than a few customers had taken him up on it, and there were five ex-cons on staff now. Five ex-cons and Mat. The turnover was high — some went back to prison while others left for a bigger city — but Kevin had stayed, and despite bets to the contrary, so had Afternoon

Shift Terry, who often had to be reminded that his grey beard needed trimming. Terry didn't listen; shift after shift his beard was longer, because Terry was his own man.

———

Regardless of its posted hours, Main Street Coffee generally closed by dinnertime. Terry had come in at noon, as usual, and joined Kevin in teasing Mat. They kept it up until after five, when Mat had finished washing the coffee makers, and as they did every night, they invited him to Gordo's, the decaying pub down the street, where they split a pitcher of beer in three glasses, filled to the brim.

It didn't take long — it never did — for Kevin and Terry to start talking about old times, throwing the odd footnote and dismissive glance toward Mat and adding, "Not like *this* fuckin' pussy would know." Terry's lazy eye was rolling all over tonight, and after another story about almost taking a shiv — almost, always almost — he trained his pupil on Mat. "Once you've nearly been shanked," Terry said, and Mat interrupted, curling his top lip: "*Your life changes in a hurry.*"

Terry stood up. "And who the fuck do you think *you* are?"

Kevin gripped Terry's arm. "Come on — down, pal," he said. He looked at Mat. "What's with you?"

Mat's pint was nearly empty. He finished it and let out a heavy breath. "It's just the same shit every day," he said. "I drag myself to work, listen to you two go on about life inside, and then I go home and eat a can of beans because Marnie won't cook for me. She can't stand the sight of me. I stay up too late watching TV, and the next morning, I wake up exhausted and do it all over again."

Terry looked at Kevin. "His wife doesn't cook."

The two of them started laughing.

"Poor baby," Kevin said. "Now meeting a guy like Big Boy Jackson, that'll change — "

"Stop it," Mat said. He stared into his glass and sniffed.

Kevin's face fell. "Are you actually going to *cry*, Matty?"

Mat looked from Kevin to Terry, who still towered over the table.

"I'm sorry, Terry, I just . . . I can't do this anymore," Mat said. He thought again of the CDs, of what Dr. Benny's capital-S secret might be. The commercials hadn't told Mat; money up front, like every good con. "I have to take control," he mumbled. It had slipped out, but it had felt good. A little louder, he asked, "You know what I mean?"

Terry reached for his beer and downed the last mouthful. He nodded and said, "Yeah." He dropped a five on the table and turned toward the door. "Got to go. Meeting the probation officer tomorrow." He trained his good eye on Mat. "You'll make it up to me, kid. Take it easy." The cold wind blew in as he left.

Kevin shuddered. "Another pitcher, Matty?" he asked. "Sounds like you need to talk."

Mat just nodded.

—

When Mat stumbled into the house, Marnie was asleep, sitting on the couch with their tabby in front of her usual nighttime TV, the show with hot lawyers and constant custody battles and grating piano music. He sat down beside her and she stirred when he put a hand on her thigh.

"What time is it?" she asked, her eyes opening slightly.

"It's late," he said. "I'm sorry I didn't call . . . I had a rough day."
Marnie looked around the room. With both hands she
pushed her brown hair back off her high cheekbones, exposing
the bags under her eyes. Mat remembered her wedding dress, the
photo on her parents' mantle of her as a toddler with cake all over
her face. She settled her gaze on him again, leaning in to examine
his bandage and scrunching her nose, smelling the beer.

"Mat, did you . . ."

"I got mugged."

Marnie took on a stern tone.

"You got mugged."

"Yeah," he said. Wan smile. "He only got my Visa — I didn't
have any cash, and I kept my phone."

"Oh, only the Visa," Marnie said, mockingly breezy. "Only
the Visa. Goddamnit, Mat. Why didn't you — "

"Why didn't I *what?*" he shot back, voice rising and hot blood
rushing into his face. "Kick his ass? So *I* could go to jail?"

"You've got to stand up for yourself," she said.

"He knocked me down! I didn't see him coming!"

"Of course you didn't," Marnie said. She looked away. "This is
exhausting. You're exhausting. I'm going to sleep."

She rose from the couch and started toward the bedroom.

Unsure what he was apologizing for, Mat said, "I'm sorry." He
stood up and pursued her. "I called and cancelled the card. And
my face will heal. Everything will be okay. Let's just go to bed — "

"Don't follow me," Marnie snapped. She yanked the door shut
behind her.

Mat raised his fist, but he stopped short of pounding on
the wood. He lowered his arm and walked away from the door,
which Marnie opened just enough to throw out pyjama pants

and a blanket before slamming it again. He gathered them and walked to the couch. The TV was still on, another episode of the lawyer show. It went to commercial, and there, to his surprise, was Dr. Benny, shamelessly imploring him to get on the self-confidence express. *Soon*, Mat thought — *I'll get on soon* — and then he lay down and pulled the scratchy blanket over himself.

—

When he woke, his palate tasted yeasty and his back hurt from the sofa's bent frame, but CDs or no CDs, he knew he should embrace the day, even if the warming weather was turning the snow to foot-soaking slop. He took the extra time to shave, to pick socks that matched and to lint-roll the cat hair off his slacks. Before leaving he opened the bedroom door and leaned over Marnie, kissing her cheek. She mumbled and pushed him away.

At work Mat and Kevin spoke little, frankly and politely as they stacked the previous day's milk crates in the back alley. They turned on all the lights and let the small lineup in. Mat's smile felt less fake today, and again Kevin stuck up for him, confirming for the second customer that hers was a half-caf. The shop had never run so well — even Terry showed up in a good mood — and when the stream of customers dried up around four thirty, Kevin said, "Let's call it." They cleaned the shop and locked the front door.

"Gordo's?" Terry asked.

Kevin said yes but Mat declined and gathered his bulky coat from the back room. He had decided to cook a nice dinner for himself and Marnie — another peace offering after another night like last night, one more fresh start but one that might take. The CDs were due tomorrow, after all. He zipped up and said good night and trudged through the slush to the small Chinese grocery downtown, all without noticing an added weight in his coat.

Scrounging for change to pay for his vegetables, he felt a different, colder metal. He paid and left, turning down the first alley he came to, and from under a mass of takeout and convenience store receipts he pulled a tiny pistol from the pocket, what he thought was called a snub-nose. He held it in his hand and stared at it for a time — too long — before he looked over his shoulder. He breathed out. No one was there. No one had seen. Not knowing what else to do with it, he replaced the gun in his pocket and carried the stray papers to a nearby can, where he quickly leafed through them before tossing them in. One slip wasn't a receipt but a note from a Main Street Coffee pad: *Need u to hold this a wile*, unsigned, in Terry's chicken scratch.

——

Mat had even used capers, but Marnie hadn't said much, just that she was more tired than usual. In her line of work, this was saying something, and Mat knew that even if he had found the nerve to ask her to really talk to him — or simply told her: *We need to talk* — she would suggest he ask someone else, a professional but not her. Her skills belonged to the correctional system. She shouldn't have to use them at home.

As a result he enjoyed the dinner and the relative silence, watching Marnie's cues: the hunger with which she attacked the food at first, then the conscious pause to show she was savouring it, not just fuelling up. When the plates were clear, he declined her half-hearted offer to clean up and told her to go relax. She gave him a small smile and, stiffly, an even smaller kiss on his cheek. Over the running water he heard the TV zap on, then the keyboard-heavy soundtrack. When he had dried his hands he heard the program's even worse end music. He walked to the living room and sat down beside her. She was struggling to stay awake. He put an arm around her shoulder. She scowled slightly but didn't push him away.

"One dinner won't fix us," she said, nearly in a sigh.

"What can I do?"

"I don't know anymore."

Mat searched her eyes a moment before she looked away, first at the ceiling and then toward the TV. She wasn't so heartless as to watch the lawyer show instead of working through this — was she? He lifted his arm off her and edged away. Her stare landed on the screen. She entered her daze.

"Honey," he said.

"Why don't you go for a walk or something?" she muttered.

"Fine, Marnie," he spat, then raising his voice, "Fine!" He got up and stomped down the hallway to the kitchen, where he took his coat from the hook and put it over his shoulders. He felt the weight in the pocket and clutched the outside of it; Kevin and Terry would have said he looked like a three-year-old discovering his cock. He stood motionless a few seconds then started back toward the living room, hand tightly gripping the contours of the pistol. He stopped in the doorway. Marnie had fallen asleep. He watched a moment. She didn't move. He stepped toward her, softly now, contemplating her a while longer, comparing the zombie she had become to the lively undergraduate she had been. He let go of the bulge and gently took the TV remote from the couch. He pressed *Off* and, stooping as little as possible so the pocket wouldn't bump her — she could *not* find out — he draped the blanket from the back of the couch over her. She didn't stir, and when he left the room, he didn't look back. The tabby didn't rouse when he opened the front door, nor when he eased it shut and strode into the frigid night.

———

He didn't know where to go first, following his street away from Main and into the large park at its end where the ice rink was lit up. Boys and girls, men and women, passed a puck back and forth, laughing and occasionally tumbling. He walked past, thinking of how he and Marnie had lived so near for four years but hadn't followed through on a single skate date. He sat down on a picnic table in a pavilion, turning his back to the rink and obscuring himself in the dark. Barely removing the gun from his pocket, he pushed the cylinder to the side. His chest constricted — Terry had loaded six bullets. All this time, Mat could have accidentally shot someone, or himself, or even Marnie when he leaned over her. That would be his luck. But he thought of his resolve, and the CDs en route. And this other stuff — the dinner, telling Kevin and Terry how he felt — this was only the beginning. Dr. Benny could well be full of shit, but he said it in the ads: *It's never too late to become your own master.* Mat rose from the picnic table and spent a moment watching the shinny hockey match. No one seemed to want to score; everyone just passed until someone literally stood on the goal line with the puck. There weren't even goalies. *Why don't they shoot?* he thought, then: *Why don't I?* The impulse made him feel sick to his stomach. He lowered his head and walked out of the park.

———

It was after midnight when he reached the main street, and increasingly he looked over his shoulder to see if anyone was following him, if anyone had noticed his sagging pocket or his fraught mind. He passed the coffee shop and unwillingly thought of shattering the windows, and in front of Gordo's he stopped to wonder whether Kevin was inside. He imagined walking in and finding his mugger there. He would start a fight; it would end with a surprise. He had enough bullets to get away, too, shooting his way out like a real man, like Newman and Redford in *Butch Cassidy* or Pacino in *Scarface*. Maybe not Pacino. He preferred imagining that Butch and the Kid got away.

The streets were quiet, even for a weeknight, and he had broken through a puddle's thin ice more than once. By the time he was downtown, his toes were freezing in his soaked boots. As little else was open, he entered a Burgerama to warm up. He anticipated a Double Beefer with equal relish and dread.

At the counter he took his wallet from his jeans, again resisting the surprising urge to draw the gun instead. *Taking down a Burgerama could be political*, he thought, remembering a news story about a bulldozer and a French McDonalds. And hadn't he just proven that he shouldn't — that everyone shouldn't — eat this slop for dinner? He'd used capers. Capers! But the indifferent clerk reminded him his bill was nine-fifty. Mat withdrew a ten from the leather and told the boy to keep the change. The boy said a sarcastic, "Thank you."

He hadn't meant to offend; really, he hadn't even meant to tip.

Now he considered shooting the kid.

*I've gone insane*, he thought.

Sitting at the table on the cold, bolted-on stool, he barely chewed the burger, devouring it with the new plan of hiding the gun in the paper wrapper and dropping the whole mess in the trash. He was the only customer in the restaurant, though, and the cashier was watching him carefully, or at least seemed to be. He might get away, but he was worried. *What if someone finds it in the trash? What if that person shoots someone? What if it's the counter boy himself? Another all-night shift at Burgerama — now there's a reason to kill someone.* He laughed to himself, but stopped. This wasn't funny. Terry would want the gun back. He had to hang on to it. He rose from the seat and cleared the tray into the bin, nicking the edge with his heavy pocket as he brushed past. He froze and swivelled his head back. Now the cashier had his nose in a guitar magazine. *He didn't see*, Mat assured himself. *He didn't see.* Thrusting his hands into his pockets, he walked out the door.

———

As always, the Double Beefer made his stomach bubble and groan. He wandered till 4:00 AM, and now found himself on the toilet at the Mega Donut near the expressway off-ramp where, to the east, the prison loomed, a floodlit block on the horizon. He had his head in his hands and was nearly retching at his own smell when someone with lazy desperation in his voice called, "Anyone in there?" and banged the door. It had become almost automatic: Mat imagined shooting in reply. He exhaled and flushed. He scanned the ceiling for cameras, thinking, *They're everywhere now*, then cursorily, *I should shoot them out.* Finding none, he put one hand in his pocket and gripped the gun as he opened the door with the other. A portly man, a trucker maybe, waited calmly with the next morning's *Star* in hand. Putting his head down and edging past, Mat barely met the man's eyes. They were vacant but somehow not burdened by the loneliest job this side of Antarctica: driving all night and day, sleeping only when — only *if* — you could afford it. The man seemed more or less content.

Mat shuddered to think he might have blindly killed him.

This had no end.

He opened the glass doors to the parking lot and stopped at a trash can outside. Cars intermittently stopped and started; headlight beams criss-crossed in all directions. He leaned against the bin, his side touching it, and thought, *Just slide it straight from your pocket.* He pushed the flap open and waited. When no lights were on him he grasped the gun with his other hand, pulling it slowly out, watching for anyone who might see him. *A piece is expensive*, he realized. *I couldn't even pay Terry for it.* He thought a moment and compromised. He could just dump the bullets. He'd slip the pistol back into Terry's coat tomorrow with a note of his own: *I'm not doing this.* Against the bottom of the bin, the first small clunk resonated and Mat's shoulders slackened. Another. A smile crept up the corners of his mouth. He didn't need the CDs — *Be Your Own Master* was working! He tilted the chamber farther into the can but froze when a car's headlights illuminated him. He squinted. Red-and-blue flashes joined the glare.

*Cops at a donut shop. Go figure.*

His first thought was to surrender.

*Typical.*

He felt an urge to put the gun to his head.

*My ultimate failure.*

And then, he heard Dr. Benny's braying voice deep in his conscience, felt it rising like a wave in his chest.

*It's never too late to become your own master — and never too early!*

He pocketed the weapon and took off sprinting, charging down a lane to the left of the shop before the officers were out of their car. He knew the streets well, and soon he was in a quiet, leafy pocket of detached houses with manicured front lawns. He slowed to a walk and made it several more blocks, zig-zagging toward home. From the main streets he heard sirens and willed his feet to speed up. He hurdled puddles and ice patches. A ten-minute run; the sirens ceased again. He was back at the park. The rink was empty and now the lights were off. He lingered in the shadows on the players' bench, staring after any potential movement and listening hard to every seeming rustle.

After a long time, he was sure he was alone.

———

He had waited so long that the sun was beginning to rise. From the park, he could see his house and the sky shifting from blue to pink beyond it. Standing up from the bench, he stretched his fingers, trying to get the blood flowing. He neared a garbage can and pulled the gun from his coat, opening the chamber and letting the last two bullets fall into his palm. He returned the pistol to his pocket and extended the ammo toward the receptacle. His jaw relaxed, his chest softened.

From behind him came a male voice.

"Police!"

He didn't look back, he just dropped the bullets and ran. If he circled the block and returned through an alley he might make it. He heard an engine start and a siren wail as he charged out of the park. He rounded the corner. He entered the alley and turned onto his narrow street, hearing the officer shout again. But he was nearly home. He lunged up the steps to his front door and screamed, "Marnie! Marnie!", fumbling in his coat pocket for his key. He grasped the gun and tried to jettison it and that's when he heard the explosion behind him, felt flesh and muscle tear in his back, fell forward. His collarbone shattered as the bullet went through and embedded itself in blood on the front door, which Marnie pulled open a moment later, wearing a stunned expression and her peach housecoat. Mat fell face down. As one officer kneeled to rip off the ski jacket, pressing down with meaty hands to stop the bleeding, a second cop rolled out the charges: " . . . Careless Use of Firearm, Possession of Weapon for a Dangerous Purpose, Carrying Concealed Weapon, Unauthorized Possession of Firearm . . . "

Mat raised his head to look up at Marnie, whose face had blanched. She was steadying herself, a hand on the door frame.

"I haven't done anything," he wheezed.

"Of course you haven't." Marnie lifted her stare to a distant point in sky.

"I — " Mat began.

"Don't try to talk," the kneeling cop said. The other one shot his partner a look before resuming: "Anything you say can be used against you . . . "

Mat pleaded to Marnie with his eyes.

Without meeting them, she said, "You should listen to them."

Two paramedics arrived and slid a backboard under him. They carried him to a gurney and began a hurried roll before jerking to a stop. Mat lifted his head a little, moaning as he glimpsed the brown truck parked close behind the ambulance. One medic yelled, "Hey!" The delivery man scurried along the sidewalk back to his vehicle, small white box still clutched under his arm. Mat struggled to sit up but the strength drained from his muscles. He exhaled lengthily. He lay back. His eyes started to close. Marnie would never sign for the CDs. Mat would never hear them. But for a second before he lost consciousness, he thought Dr. Benny might be proud of him.

# Tender Port

$\mathcal{S}$teve had hiked Tobermory and camped Algonquin and canoed Temagami, taking long bus trips with a high school geography class, a church youth group, and a scout troop from Waterloo, where he had lived with his parents until almost two years ago, when he finished university. He hadn't had floormates or roommates, or even met many classmates, and hadn't taken the cliché spring break in the Dominican or backpacked Europe after graduation. He hadn't even been on an airplane — the last four years, his only travels had been on the cheap to Montreal, the Greyhound's Friday overnight milk run, to see Rachel, his girlfriend since high school, at McGill.

But it was over with Rachel now, and Steve had worked straight through since the summer split at his first grown-up job, a low-level position in a bank office in Toronto, piling up the vacation days he had once stretched weekends with. The final week of January had at long last come, and he was escaping on a cruise out of Fort Lauderdale, a last-minute deal chosen after all the travel sites had begun to look the same. After booking, he had told his best friend Mike (now living in Vancouver) on Google Chat, and Mike had written back a block of *hahahahaha* so long that he had to have used copy-paste.

# HAMBURGER

*Your first vacation, he wrote, and seriously?? I know you need to get away, see someplace new, or maybe just have some meaningless sex, get yourself back on the horse, but you choose a cruise from Florida, the tackiest place on Earth?? Did you get the Disney one? Cuz otherwise you'll be the youngest one on the boat — not even any yummy single mummies to bust your slump! What were you thinking???*

Steve knew he wasn't the best-looking guy — his nose had been broken twice, both times in AAA hockey — but he had grown out his brown hair a bit and it was starting to loop behind his ears. He had never had meaningless sex — at least, none that had been meaningless to him.

———

Florida was hot but finding transport to his ship was easy, as each cruise line had signs and staff leading people to the correct minibus. He was off to a good start. Steve's ride blasted out conditioned air when he pulled open the side door. Beside the last remaining seat, a nearly bald man with a thick grey mustache barked, "Hurry up, you're letting the heat in!" Steve sat down among eight people at least the man's age, all of whom were talking about United, Delta, and Southwest; Newark, Salt Lake City and Houston. Steve put his earbuds in. The bus started rolling and his shuffling playlist hit "Livin' on a Prayer." It was cheesy but it carried good and bad memories, most of them of the karaoke bar where he and his friends had drunk underage before going their separate ways. Usually, he skipped the track, but wasn't he taking a cruise? Hadn't he come to party?

The balding man tapped his shoulder.

"Sorry. I'll turn it down," Steve mumbled.

"Turn it down?" the man said with a slight drawl. "Hell, take the headphones *out*! I *love* Bon Jovi!"

Steve tried not to stare at his neighbour's beer gut, the blindingly pale bottom of which stuck out beneath his Hawaiian shirt.

"I'm Mel," the man said, looking down at Steve's backpack on the floor and its flag patch. "*Canada*," Mel said. "Eh?" He laughed. "Gonna get some better weather now!"

Steve smiled and said, "Huh. Yeah." Mike had been right: everyone was going to be just like Mel . . . and the women would be like the plump, badly dyed blonde reading a vampire novel beside him. Ten days together, he thought. Seven ports of call: Coopman's Cay, San Juan, St. Barts, St. John's, St. Thomas, and Nassau. The seventh was Fort Lauderdale, home port, which Steve didn't count but American Queen Cruises seemed to. On the blonde's lap sat an AQ-branded shopping bag.

"Lucy and I," Mel said, "we like to get the souvenirs out of the way first then see the sights after. 'Course, Fort Lauderdale, we didn't see much. We thought we'd have time to go over to the beach for a swim, but you know how it goes."

Steve nodded and turned up the volume in his earbuds. Mel kept right on talking, to everyone and no one in the van.

—

They left the bus and joined the line at the gangplank. A staffer in a blue-and-white-striped shirt and a yellow AQ cap shouted into a megaphone, seeming to forget it existed to amplify.

"This line is for Eastern Caribbean Cruise only." An accent, maybe Cuban, was barely noticeable through the feedback. "If jou are taking the Southern Jewel cruise, go to the other platform."

# Hamburger

She repeated the instructions, at three-minute intervals, six times before Steve reached the front of the line. A male agent said, "Welcome aboard the *Margarita*," and handed him a pamphlet, a key card in a sleeve marked 309 and a postcard-sized piece of paper reading *You Are Cordially Invited To Our Opening Ceremony.* Steve flipped the card over: *8:00 PM in your deck's ballroom. This introductory meeting is mandatory.*

"The bar will be open," the agent said, waving him through. "See you after you get settled in."

—

When the boat departed, no one waved to him from shore. He changed his shirt in his room then joined the other passengers at the meeting, which covered ship rules, safety, and customs laws in the ports of call. "Final thing," said the manager. "We don't want to leave anybody behind, but if we have to, we will . . . and from what I hear, the jails in San Juan are none too nice." Steve's ballroom laughed, as he was sure the one on every deck did; as predicted, the boat was full of Mels and Lucys, their hair grey or gone, waists and ages forty and up. He scanned the room and saw just one woman in the room who could pass for thirty-five, an obvious trophy wife clinging to the arm of a white-haired man in a tuxedo. *Nice work, Viagra.*

Eventually, Steve settled into an armchair by a porthole. He looked out into the night sea's infinite black, and polished off his complimentary Jack-and-Coke. In the morning, there would be nine days till he had to go back to work. It depressed him to be already thinking about work. He rose from the seat, which was overstuffed and uncomfortable, and slunk down the hall to his room.

# Tender Port

—

He slept in, and barely made it to the breakfast buffet before it closed. Lined up with thirty Mels, he dodged palm-tree-print bellies and arms lunging furiously for the last sausages. He checked the schedule while he scarfed his scrambled eggs and was surprised to see how little time they had on Coopman's Cay; sure, it was a small island, but back to the ship by six? He finished his plate, hustled to his room, and put on his swim trunks. He unfolded a canvas day bag and packed quickly: sunscreen, his room towel, iPod and earbuds, and two novels. He wouldn't read them both, but he preferred to have options — Rachel had been the same way, packing twenty outfits for Christmas holidays at home, where she still had a full closet of clothes.

He descended to the lower deck and watched the craft approach. It was orange and white, with a closed top, and shaped kind of like a hovercraft he'd seen in an old James Bond movie. The group he boarded with was mostly flabby, goateed men in open, flame-print polyester button-ups and their tramp-stamped, muffin-topping wives. All had sweaty bags under their boozy eyes. He held the rail as the trip started, and not ten minutes later, the American Queen shop on shore came into focus, crammed no doubt with shot glasses, playing cards, collectible spoons, and everything else people only buy on vacation.

As he disembarked, the crew explained the brightly painted boardwalks: a short blue one, with clear signage in huge letters reading SHUFFLEBOARD; an orange one leading to the bar, which took care of most of his boatmates; a pink one to Activities Cove®, and a green one for the plain old beach.

Steve chose green. He laid his towel on the ground. The sun was hotter, the sand whiter, the air less humid than Wasaga,

Woodbine, or the tiny, bone-chilling lakes in northern Ontario he'd forgotten the names of, but overall, a beach was a beach. There was nothing to do but apply sunscreen, swim, reapply sunscreen and look at the scenery. It all reminded him of *Death in Venice*, most of which he had read while getting his mandatory arts credit. Women had squeezed wide hips, extraneous rolls, and sagging breasts into one-piece swimsuits, while most of the men wore T-shirts into the water. He was beginning to understand von Ass' fixation on the boy. But this had to be better than staying on the ship, didn't it? On land he had at least a chance of seeing something that hadn't arrived via Florida. He stared down the length of the beach; there had to be somewhere he could get off the beaten track. He thought of asking a staffer, but he knew he'd just be redirected to Activities Cove to try scuba diving, or parasailing, or just hop on the catamaran . . . In his head the employees shilled like the actors on his room TV's default channel.

There was only beaten track here.

—

After a dip in the water TravelHub.net had called "calm" and "ideal for swimming," he sagged into a long, white beach chair. He rummaged in his bag for either *Robinson Crusoe* or *For Whom the Bell Tolls*, two doorstops he had attempted before but abandoned. He wound up with the Hemingway and opened to the epigraph; he had never heard of John Donne, but apparently, the writer believed that every man's death diminished him, because he too was part of "Mankinde." He seemed to think Europe poorer when even an idiot drowned. Steve lifted his eyes and surveyed everyone lazing around him. Maybe he was being too hard on the other passengers. The bell would toll for them soon enough — very soon, in some cases — but wasn't it tolling for him, too? He should have some fun while he still could! There was, after all, *scuba diving, and paddle-boarding, and even a water-slide* . . .

And a pair of beautiful legs walking right past him, in navy shorts cut well above the knee.

He stuck his nose back in the book, but not his eyes, which were hidden by sunglasses. He followed the legs up to a torso, a blue-and-white-striped American Queen T-shirt, and a big purse bursting at the seams. He wondered whether she had noticed him too. He thought about his pasty skin, his body that betrayed his lack of gym motivation. His nose-bump might play, though; he'd enjoyed explaining hockey to the (very) few American women he'd met. It could be fun to help a Bahaman — *Bahamian? It's Bahamian* — imagine Canada's insane death match on ice.

He caught himself staring. *Hate to see you go, love to watch you walk away* played through his mind, but he didn't love that on the first day the most beautiful woman he'd see all trip was already leaving him. He snatched up his bag in one hand, the flip-flops he had kicked off in the other, and set off down the beach at a jog. Nearer to her, he slowed to a walk that matched her purposeful pace and let his breathing slow. It wasn't like him to just approach a woman like this — or was it? Until half a year ago, he'd been in the same relationship since the tenth grade. He had no idea what was like him.

"Excuse me!"

She turned back. The skin on her face was smooth and her eyebrows finely styled; *Angela* was embroidered on the shirt, and a lanyard rested between her perfect breasts. She squinted into the sun behind him.

"Yes?"

Her voice was low — self-assured and a little annoyed.

"I'm looking for something to do," Steve said. "I mean, somewhere to go. Something to see. Is there a town?"

Angela scoffed. "Here? You must be kidding." She said it like *kid din*.

"No, I'm not. I mean, how do people live here? Where do people eat?"

"No one *lives* here, Mister — "

"Steve," he offered.

"Mister Steve," she said flatly. "People just stay."

"All year long?"

Recognition flashed in her dark eyes. "*You*'ve never taken a cruise before."

Steve shook his head.

"American Queen owns this island," she said. "We get you off and on your boat, we make you food and drinks, and we clean up after you when you leave. Then we go over that hill" — she pointed in the direction she had been walking — "to our cabins and we sleep. We do it every day for a few months, then we get tired of it and go home." It seemed like a speech she had given before. "Excuse me," she added, making to leave. "It's actually my day off."

"Sorry," Steve said. "You were wearing your uniform, I just assumed."

"You would."

"What?" He didn't understand what he had done wrong.

"Maybe not *you*," she said. "But people like you. You don't know nothing."

She put no *h* in nothing; *no-ting.*

"So teach me."

She raised her eyebrows at him, like he'd called her a rude name. "I don't think so." She turned her back to him and took a step toward the hill.

"Good thing it's your day off," Steve said. "Otherwise they'd fire you."

She swivelled her head and fixed the dark eyes on him. They softened some. "I wasn't that bad," she said.

"Nah." Steve smiled a little. "You weren't. And I get it. I'll go ask someone else." He turned to walk away but stopped. "But why are you in your work clothes?"

"I'm not going to tell you that," she said.

He flashed a cockier grin. "Could I change your mind?"

"What is it you want from me?"

"I want to get to know you," he said. "I want to do things together."

"Things," she said. *Tings.* She laughed and looked at her watch. "It's after two. You have four hours — less, even." She scowled a little. "I don't get paid for that, by the way."

"I want to see where you stay, how you have fun."

"*I'm* not part of the package," she said.

"No," Steve said. "You're not." He thought a moment. He couldn't let her go. "We'd be . . . " — it sounded desperate but he said it anyway — "We'd be friends."

She stared at him a long time.

The path up the sandy hill eventually disappeared into trees, tall palms that the sun streaked though.

"It's beautiful," Steve said. "Thanks for bringing me here."

"I told you, I'm not your tour guide."

She said it with a smile, though.

"What do you do on your day off?"

"Normally I try to be left alone."

"Me too," Steve said. "Do you take off to another island? Can you even do that? Are there boats?"

"You said you wanted to be my friend," she said. "You sound like my six-year-old nephew."

"Can I meet him?"

"Ha-ha," she said. "Funny boy. My family's in Nassau, you'll see them there."

Steve cocked his head.

She puffed up and deepened her voice. "When you climb up to Fort Fincastle, ignore all the pirate stories and look over the hill — *away* from the water, at the rusted roofs and burned-out cars and blue-and-orange tarps. It's our dog barking, the yelling is my parents fighting, the revving moped is my no-good brother, and the smoke, that's our cook fire — " Her smile, growing the whole speech, gave way to a laugh.

"I get it," Steve said, laughing, too. "Ignorant white boy."

They came out the other side of the trees in front of a row of rundown structures, not cabins so much as shacks. There were weedy gardens in front of them, and at the end of the row, a chewed-up football pitch with no nets on the rotting wood goals.

"You live *here*?" Steve asked.

"I'm afraid so."

"But all the other buildings . . . "

"All the new buildings are for you. We get the police barracks that were abandoned when their new complex was built a couple islands over — with the money American Queen paid for this one, no less."

She unlocked the gate and entered the grounds. She led him into the small clapboard building, which had a newer looking exterior than some. It was a basic bachelor apartment inside, minus a few things.

"No kitchen?"

Angela shook her head, holding up the lanyard and plastic card at its end. "We eat in the restaurant," she said. "We have a daily limit." She opened the shutters and let the musty air out. The breeze off the water blew in. "Okay, go now," she said. "You know I eat the same as you, and you've seen where I live."

She sounded serious. Then she started laughing. "Just go outside for a minute."

He stared at her.

She put a hand just above his hip and gave him a little push. "Go."

He waited outside a few minutes before the door opened. She was now wearing a loose-fitting yellow blouse, a purple bikini top and green shorts, much shorter than the uniform ones. She carried a smaller faux-leather purse.

"That's better," she said.

"Same clothes all night . . . ?"

She took a quick look in her purse. "All right, I'm ready. Let's go to the beach."

"I didn't love it there . . . "

"I mean the people's beach."

---

There were no windsurfers, no sign-up lists for horseback rides at sunset, no offers to braid women's hair. Skiffs came and went, people fished, and fires burned on the beach to cook the day's catch. No one was swimming.

"Everyone here works for American Queen," Steve asked. "Right?"

"Most of them. Though some just drift up out of nowhere." She breathed out and said, "I hate this island."

"Why'd you come here?"

"Money," she said. "I have a diploma, but I can only get jobs in tourism."

"No tourists in Nassau?"

"Nassau's home — it's real. At least, away from the wharf it is. I can't sell it the way they tell me to." She practically spat the next word: "Atlantis." She rolled her eyes. "Off the boat, get your day pass, go back drunk at night and say you've seen The Bahamas. At least Coopman's was built to be fake."

"So what should I do to really see The Bahamas?"

She laughed. "The Bahamas. It's only us and The Gambia still need a 'the' in our name." She looked far out into the sea. "There are more than seven hundred islands," she said. "You don't see The Bahamas — The Bahamas is some white guy's idea."

"That's kind of like 'Canada,'" Steve said, making quotes with his hands. "Toronto isn't like Vancouver Island . . . and Quebec is kind of its own planet . . . and then there are the Indian Reserves, which we don't like to talk about . . ."

She didn't seem to be listening. She sighed. "I have a boyfriend," she said. "Sort of. He's a supply boat captain, a German guy."

"Oh."

"He comes through once a week. We meet on his boat after my shift. We just had a fight about why I won't move to Florida with him." She almost shuddered. "*Florida*."

"I hear you."

She wagged a finger. "So no funny business."

"Of course." She stared toward the shore. Steve followed her gaze to a man removing a hook from a fish's mouth.

"Having a tourism job but still wanting to catch your supper," she said. "If *The Bahamas* is anything, it's something like that."

———

They were well into the afternoon, and Steve hadn't eaten since the ship.

"Will he sell any of his catch?"

"He'll give you some if you just ask," she answered.

Embarrassed, Steve clammed up. It seemed wrong to buy the man's fish, but much worse to ask him for it. He dipped into *Robinson Crusoe*, which was as boring as he remembered, and an awkwardness hung over them for twenty or thirty minutes. But when he could read absolutely no more, he looked up and the unease seemed to have blown away. They talked about American movies they had both seen, places they wanted to travel, whether they wanted kids someday. When Steve saw five twenty on his watch, he felt sadness in addition to a little panic.

"We have to go," he said. "What if I miss the boat?"

"Big trouble, Mister Steve." Angela smiled. "Though you'd have a good reason."

He was melting inside, remembering finally: it's so damned easy to fall in love.

"Relax," she said as they gathered their things and began walking. "The boat's on Island Time."

"Island Time." Steve laughed. He had heard it somewhere; it meant everything was a bit late. "So that's real?" he asked.

"We aren't allowed to call it Drunk Tourist Time."

As they emerged from the trees, he took her hand. It was soft inside his. She didn't pull away, didn't seem to react at all.

"So," she said. "Coopman, San Juan, St. Barts, St. John's, St. Thomas . . . then Nassau, right?"

"Yeah," Steve said. "You've got to tell me what to do there. I won't get too far in — "

"No, don't," she said.

"But the fort, right?"

"See the fort if you must." She laughed. "But when you get up there, look down at your ship and the others like it. Compare how big they are to the size of the city."

"I will," Steve said.

"And take the sixty-five steps when you go down."

"The Queen's Staircase?" He had read about it on the internet.

"Yes."

"Carved for Queen Victoria, right?"

She pulled back her hand. "*Named* for Victoria. Built by slaves who worked *sixteen years* to give the English a faster way down to the water."

"Oh."

"They were named later, when slavery was abolished."

Foot-in-mouth again. Embarrassment rose in Steve's chest, gripping the base of his throat. They walked in silence the last minutes to the dock where the little orange boat waited.

"I'll watch for your family," he said, unsure whether it should be a joke.

She smiled and replied, "Look hard."

They locked eyes a moment, then she leaned in and kissed him on the cheek. The deckhands stared, and the bleary-eyed couples from the morning, drunk again, cheered from the boat. Angela covered her face and laughed.

"I'm so glad I met you," he said, voice breaking a little. He walked up the gangplank and to the front of the tender, where a smile crept up his cheeks. He had doubly struck out on Mike's challenge: he hadn't had sex, and so far, his experience hadn't been meaningless, either. He leaned on the railing and watched the *Margarita* come into view. It cast its shadow over the smaller craft two full minutes before they would dock, and for the first time, he recognized the ship's immensity.

# Aria di Gelato

*I* quit smoking on my fortieth birthday, when I saw that tombstone in my mind: *Giuseppe Parolini, 1985-2025*. It just didn't seem long enough.

That was four years ago, before they found cancer in my lungs. I mean, you always know you could die tomorrow, but these days, it's true. I could go anytime.

My son Joe's stayed with me everyday for the last two months, and if I take much longer to die, he might lose his job. But Joey will be all right. The world might not need me anymore, but it's still going to need bricklayers for a while. I mean, they're expensive, and they're a pain in the ass, but brick houses still can't be mass-produced. Somebody's always got to get up in the morning and put up the walls, brick by goddamned brick.

Now these hospitals, on the other hand, they're mass-producing old people. I told Joey a long time ago that when the day comes, it'll have to be him who pulls the plug. In fact, I asked for a natural death, which to me seems like not even hooking up the respirator in the first place. But no, everybody still thinks they're killing somebody if they're not helping them live.

I'll tell you one thing, though. If it's between death and an unnatural life, I'd rather the first. There are just so many machines here keeping me alive.

# Aria di Gelato

This one beeps when my heart rate's down.

That one watches my white blood cells.

The one over by the window, though, that one's new. The nurse wheeled it in last week and asked Joe if he'd like to test out a new Patient Services project with me. He's tried to ask my permission, but I'm too weak now to say anything. The machine works kind of like that thing Stephen Hawking used, only I don't have to type. Not that I was ever much good with that. It spits out what I'm saying without my having to breathe, which is a good thing, considering. In a nutshell, it translates the brain's electrical impulses, or at least that's what the nurse told Joe when they thought I was asleep. They always think I'm asleep, and lately I've been pretending a lot, thinking it might help Joey get used to the idea. Poor kid's a mess.

Joe's been staring at the machine all week, though, and I think he's finally made up his mind. So when he whispers "Papa" today, I force my eyelids open.

He's twenty-two. He hasn't called me that in a decade.

"Papa, we got to try this," Joe says, holding up the headgear. "I got to know what you're thinking. I got to know that it's right. Can we do this, Papa?"

I can't even nod, so I just tap his forearm with one finger. He looks up at the ceiling and says, "*Grazie*," and puts the headband on me.

Joey already knows how I feel about the whole euthanasia thing, though — so now that I've got him listening, I should tell him this instead.

—

So back when I'm a young man, I'm working in this menswear store in Dufferin Mall. Hardest-working neighbourhood in Toronto. It's a hot night in the summertime and the mall's full, 'cause it's got air conditioning, so let's say it's a Monday. Yeah, sure, it's a Monday when I hear this song.

In front of the store we've got this big table of folded sweaters, and customers are walking by picking them up. You know, trying them on, trying to steal them, whatever.

So this table, it's always a mess. I *hate* folding these sweaters. I work so slowly, come to think of it, I don't know why they don't fire me. I mean, I'm always looking out into the other stores, watching the girls go by with their overdone curls and their push-up bras, you know what I'm talking about.

So it's Monday night, and in the concourse there's this guy, a father, leading his two little girls around. The older one's probably four, the younger one's, I don't know, two? Maybe less. And I'm kind of surprised, because I grew up here so I should know this guy, but I don't.

Anyway, he's about thirty, wearing this black baseball cap and a polo, five o'clock shadow like any good Eyetie, and he's got this ice cream cup. He squats down to his younger daughter and he holds out this pink plastic spoon and he says, "Here, Honey. Have some ice cream." Even from where I'm standing I know it's chocolate. I can see the shadow through the white paper cup. And under *these* fluorescent lights? I can see it even through the *spoon*.

Well, as if he has to tell her twice, she gives this little smile, *truly* grateful, like only little kids can be, and she bites into the ice cream without using her little teeth. You know. One. Quick. Taste.

# Aria di Gelato

Now, I'm watching this dad giving his little girl ice cream, so I don't see the old man on four legs walk up behind them. (Yeah, two of his own and two metal crutches hooked up to his arms.) But I *hear* him coming. And I realize, actually, that I had heard him coming before I even saw the dad with the little girls, because what got me looking out of the store in the first place was this whistling I could hear.

And this isn't just any whistling. He's not coming out of the bathroom or filling a weird silence or anything. It's, I don't know, *musical*. Huh, yeah, I remember. There's all this stuff going on in the mall: parents are dragging screaming kids around, teenagers are threatening each other and chasing each other and breaking up. You know. But all *I* can hear is this guy, whistling. And I mean, I don't know anything about music, but this guy's on key. I can just tell from the sound because it's so deep and full of life, like, I don't know, the Nile River or something.

I told you this guy is old. But seriously, he must be about eighty-five, and other than his crutches and lips I don't think he can *move* anything else. But when he's whistling, he looks like he's putting his mouth around some kind of invisible mouthpiece, like on a clarinet or something. He moves his eyes a little too, I remember. He looks at the little girl and there's this spark in his eyes. It's like it's faded, but it's never gone away.

So now I'm just standing there, in front of my folding table, checking if anyone else is paying attention. This woman almost comes out of the store beside ours but her husband steps lightly on her foot. He looks at his wife, then looks at the man and the little girl, and his wife knows she'd better look too.

It's like that on-the-spot theatre you see on TV sometimes, improv or whatever it's called. People are all over the place, passing by, not looking up or anything, but this old guy, he's playing this concert. *For five people*: me, and the couple next door, and the two-year-old, and her dad.

The four-year-old, I don't know what she's looking at. Something on the roof I guess.

Anyway, to us it was like everything else went quiet. Everybody says you could hear a pin drop, but Joey, you could have heard less than that. I *swear* to you, there was nothing in this mall other than this old guy and this little girl. It's theory of relativity or something, right? Time only moves as fast as the guy watching it go by? Sounds right, because I'm standing perfectly still and time, Joey, time is *stopping*.

There's probably sixty people around him who *should* be hearing this and there's five, maybe six, that are listening. You know, *really* listening.

And the song this guy is playing! It's slow, and it's sad, and the sound, it's . . . rich, like the ice cream the father's wiping off the two-year-old's chin. And I mean I don't know if this old guy's Italian or not, but this song, every note's just sadder than the last one and it just makes me think about Verona, and cobblestones, and my nonno going on about going to the opera with *his* nonno . . . Ah shit, you know what, Joey, I never did get over there.

So this old guy's whistling his song, but he hasn't even stopped walking yet. Not like he's moving fast or anything, but he stops and bends down — picture it, he's eighty-five and he's bending down to a two-year-old — and he balances his crutches somehow and he doesn't fall.

He holds out his hand to the little girl. She tries to grab it, but he smiles and he pulls it away and he puts it in his pocket, like he's playing peekaboo or something. She's pouting and I think, *Oh no, now she's going to cry*, but what does he do? He pulls this little blue-and-white box out of his pocket. And inside it he's got this harmonica.

Now he looks like a warrior, taking his sword out of his sheath. But it's not for king or country or anything like that, it's bigger. He takes this huge breath in, he puts the thing up to his lips, and he starts playing for the little girl.

It's thick. And clear. It . . . *resonates*.

So of course she starts to dance. She's got this dark hair, long for a two-year-old and already starting to curl, and it's just bouncing to the beat. Not the beat of the song, I don't think, just . . . whatever beat she's feeling. You know kids.

Anyway, I think he plays about as long as a TV commercial and when he finishes he's all smiles and everything. The silence breaks up and I start hearing the other sounds again, the crying babies and the ringing cell phones and the big bass coming from the record store and right then I know: this is something I'm never going to forget.

But you know, Joey, the song itself? I've got no idea how that goes. Maybe I could have hummed it on the way home that night, but it's long gone now.

Like I was saying, the old man finishes playing and he smiles at the little girl. He takes an extra second to look into her little brown eyes and then he starts to hobble away. And this guy, he is in *pain*. So all I can think is, *Where did this guy find the breath for this?*

You know, Joey, I never spoke much Italian, and I think your nonno might still have been mad about that when he died. But I remember some. *Respirare*. Respire, if that's a word. It means breathe. Breathe in, it's *inspirare*, and breathe out, it's *espirare*. Hundreds of times a day, inspire and expire. I remember thinking that was kind of funny when I was a kid, but now it just feels so . . . sad, you know?

And the guy, broken-down legs and worn-out face and even his clothes look like they're retired, he's passing something on. Like from the past *over* the present, straight to the future. I don't know, I think . . . I think all that was left of him was his heart. I guess that's where it came from, because for that moment, right when he put the harmonica to his lips, we were all like the little girl looking at the ice cream on the pink spoon, just waiting to pounce and eat it all in one bite.

So anyway, the old guy's gone and I look at the dad, who's stopped in front of me and my table of two-for-twenty-dollar sweaters, and I start thinking I'm missing something — that this guy's just the girls' nonno and everybody's been out shopping together all day.

So I ask, "Do you know that guy?"

The dad, he's actually wiping a tear, he just shakes his head and says, "No."

The two-year-old's tugging on his sleeve. She wants more ice cream. It's all melted now.

And you know what? It's only quarter-to-nine. I've still got fifteen minutes to kill at this damn sweater table. So I go back to the stock room, I get the broom, and after we close I walk all the way up to Davenport to your mother's parents' house and stand on the porch. And when she gets to the door? I ask her to marry me.

Anyway, that's it, Joey. I don't know if you remember. When you were a baby I used to whistle to you all the time.

# Aria di Gelato

—

These fluorescent lights are so bright. Joey's hair's all messy and the poor kid's got tears drawing lines down his cheeks. He takes off the headset and goes to the door, but stops beside the light switch. He looks back at me.

I force a smile and rasp it out. "Off."

He nods.

"Sleep well, Papa. I'll go get the doctor."

The room goes dark.

# Vaporetto

My three-year-old, Ethan, stood up on my lap, pressed his feet into my thighs and — green sippy cup falling from his hand — pushed off like a gymnast toward the boat's yellow railing. I flung an arm between the American torsos and caught his wrist, but this lady, this fat cow, slapped me and yelled nasally, "*Polizia!*" I lost my grip for just a second, and when I clasped again my fingers found only my palm. Fatso's face blanched and I heard a few screams. I shouldered her and stepped onto the railing. I dove over the side. The sludgy water filled my shoes and I sank — eyes open, stinging — as I looked for his blond curls, his Osh Kosh. I thought I saw him rising and followed him up, but I surfaced alone in the waterbus' wash. The hot sun beat down and I tasted the murk. Already, a blue-and-white police craft was motoring up, its mustached pilot scribbling a fifty-euro swimming ticket.

"*Inglese!*" I called. "My son! *Mio*" — I searched for the word — "*figlio!*" I pivoted in every direction, looking for Ethan. I yelled at the cop again, and this time he took a radio from his belt clip and machine-gunned Italian into the mouthpiece. He gestured to the canal bank. Outboards pull-started and colleagues scrambled into wetsuits; the filth still chilled in April, a cold that only hit once treading had exhausted me. My mouth and nose filled with the stench my numb toes stirred up. The cop pulled me over the gunwale, and another draped a blanket over my shoulders. From the small deck I watched the divers flop into the brown and green, the stink and muck and shit — actual shit — plunging again and again to the canal's diseased bottom.

———

Michelle and I had wanted to go to Italy for years, and had spent three months meticulously planning, an hour or two most nights once Ethan was in bed. But before we left: Lyndsay. Lyndsay with no business scrawling her name, never mind enrolling in a Creative Writing program. Then again, BFA: Bachelor of Fuck All. I never got one, I just wrote short stories — two small-press manifestoes two years apart, barely notable enough to get me in on a young Toronto university's new cash-grab. Given ten years, I became the longest-tenured instructor[1]. I didn't get a say in Lyndsay's admission, but I'm told she had a recommendation from Cheryl Chabert, that perfectly bilingual, three-time Giller Prize-winning blurbosaur who apparently says nothing but *world-opening, full of splendour, magnifique*. The lines are never true but they sell books anyway. Take a few such superlatives, add an autograph for the English Department archive, and of course Lyndsay gets in.

———

Did you ever see a grown woman actually bat her eyelashes? Blonde and not overly tall, Lyndsay's hips and breasts curved just enough to make her soft, and inviting. And then there were the eyelashes: coquettish, in a word, though I can't say I like that one. She was the perfect little fool Daisy Buchanan dreamed

---

[1] Not to be confused with having tenure.

of. And while *Never judge a book by its cover* is a wise saying, I prefer *Sleeping with your students isn't worth it, because afterward you'll have to read their short stories.* A week later in the morning workshop, the one that I didn't teach, Lyndsay went right for my misogynist throat (her word, not mine), presenting a piece about a disappointing night "Laura" spent with her writing teacher. My other students said it was god-awful work, but it connected with the guest instructor that day, Michelle Melanson, who was fresh off the success of her Italian-set, 600-page, Governor-General's-Award-nominated *Love in the Time of Cholera* rip-off, and who happened, at the time, to be my wife.

———

We were supposed to travel together, with Ethan, but after that class, unbeknownst to me[2], Michelle changed the travel dates. When they left, I was already on suspension and, for the first time in years, spending whole days in the library, poring over journal articles about Dostoyevsky and Salinger and how to create sympathy for an unlikeable narrator. I came home with a stack of books under one arm and I knew when no one answered my "Michelle . . . ?" that I wouldn't need to open the dining room table letter, had she left one. Everything of Ethan's was gone from the bathroom cupboards: training pants, talcum powder, baby versions of sunscreen and shampoo and bug repellent. This last item clinched it. Standing water breeds mosquitoes — swirling around staleness, seeking new blood. She had taken him straight to Venice.

———

———

[2] Forgive the cliché.

# Vaporetto

It was morning when I landed in Rome and, like I would have with Michelle and Ethan, I rode the shuttle to Termini. We'd have stayed for three days of Trevi Fountain and Colosseum before validating our rail pass and leaving for Cinque Terre's cliffs, then Milan and Turin, and we'd have eaten our way through Emilia-Romagna — Bolognese, Modenese, Reggiano, Parmigiana — before our guest reading at the Italian Writers' Union in Venice, then Florence and *David* and Rome's airport again, finally. But alone at the crowded automatic wickets, all I booked was a one-way to Santa Lucia Venezia Station, where I stepped out four hours later. Over the Grand Canal, the Scalzi Bridge reflected the sun in blinding white. I reminisced a moment about Michelle always insisting that Ethan wear his tiny shades.

The map was a challenge but finding her wouldn't be. Giving up a room this time of year meant sleeping on the street. The website had said the Hotel Giardino was near the Rialto, the way to which was pointed by yellow signs with black arrows. I followed them the long way, around the canal — when all the while I could have cut across the Scalzi to the city centre, I found out later — and my carry-on thundered on the cobblestones as I nudged and wedged and shoved through the crowds, up and down staircases over countless miniature bridges until I arrived sweaty and red-faced at the hotel. I gave Michelle's name at the front desk and the clerk looked down his pointed nose at me. She was staying there, he confirmed in broken English, but had asked that my calls not be forwarded. He didn't see an in-person call any differently. I left and in front of the Giardino's picture window I made a four-dollar-a-minute call, my cell to hers. She didn't pick up, but she never went a day without checking it. I returned the phone to my pocket and thought of what to do next. She could only be two places, inside or out, so I walked to the bar terrace across the street — a tourist trap if I've ever seen one — and chose a table facing the hotel. The waiter offered me a spritz, some big drink here, orange and ice-cold and served bitter or sweet. I chose the former and ordered another each time my glass emptied, keeping my eyes glued to the Giardino. Four times the black-uniformed clerk stepped out to smoke; he noticed me on the third, and the final time shook his head and looked at his feet, muttering.

I was nearly out of euros when Michelle turned up, pushing the stroller, her red hair frazzling slightly in the late afternoon humidity. I tossed thirty on the table and called her name as I walked toward her. She turned and let out a small cry. Ethan lolled his head backward but stayed asleep.

"What are you doing here?" Her voice was a shouted whisper.

I had waited over two hours without readying an answer — and had she been any later, I'd have been drooling drunk, too. All I said was, "You didn't have to go."

She exhaled sharply[3] through her nose and angled the stroller toward the hotel. Ethan stirred again.

"Hey, buddy," I said.

His tongue began forming a "Da — "

"Don't you dare put him in the middle," she said, wheeling away without looking back at me. She grabbed the door handle.

"It's kidnapping, Michelle."

She stopped and whirled, green eyes wide.

"We'll see what the court says."

"And until then?"

---

[3] Can I still say this? I hear it's all over *Fifty Shades of Grey.*

# Vaporetto

She pulled the door and dashed through the opening, the chime tinkling behind her. At the counter, the clerk smirked through the window and shrugged. I flicked my right hand at him from under my chin and returned to the table across the street. I was already reaching for my MasterCard.

— —

The short version puts Michelle in one of my workshops — my stables, she called them after she became the latest female student to learn the hard way there's nothing to gain screwing the instructor. The long version tells you she was doe-eyed in the usual way, but older — thirty-two — and a competent writer more than capable of calling me on my bullshit. We didn't converse or even properly fuck; we sparred, competing always, each trying to bend the other to his[4] will, and gleeful every time we moved in for the pin, gloating where passion should have been. She found my female characters too pliant, too invisible, and she'd tease me about it while she perched on my hips, saying once we were married, "You don't get a vote: I'm making this baby." Other guys with kids had told me it sinks in for her the moment she finds out — that no matter how many pre-natal anythings a man attends, no matter how much nursery renovating or how many foot massages, a father isn't fully aware what he's signed up for until the little face in the blanket looks back at him. It was all I could do not to drop Ethan then, when suddenly it — all of it — was no longer about me. Once I had a hold, I decided I would never let him go. Not until the day he broke free.

— —

---

[4] Pronouns, pronouns.

# Hamburger

A thirteenth hotel had turned me away, and now it was night. The fish market on the dark side of the Rialto was filled with young people, their hands gripping brown and green glass litres, or white paper cups with two gelato flavours per, tasted from translucent plastic *cucchiai*[5]. Electronic music thumped from a bar's open front and echoed in the vaulted sidewalks. I passed a pay phone and thought about it, but she wouldn't have heard a word, so I circled the block so as not to look lost near ordinary Venetians, the only people here more hostile to tourists than hotel clerks. I crossed back over the bridge, not stopping even to see the light and shadow along the canal banks, the moon that ghosted the sinking city while in the distance a gondolier sang , "'O Sole Mio'', the number one request, never mind that it's a Neapolitan song. My phone vibrated — free Wi-Fi on the bridge — and the messages I had missed since leaving home piled in. I stepped into the first joint at the bottom of the stairs, a take-off on a 1930s New York jazz club, and sat at the bar and ordered a bottle of Moretti. The most recent email was from Michelle and said only, *It was good of you to come. I'm in room 208.* I looked completely the crude North American as I snatched up the beer and slurped it while I rushed across the Sestiere San Marco. I yanked the hotel door open and looked around the lobby for the way up.

The clerk moved to block me, drawing out, "*Signore?*" as though scolding a puppy. Didn't this fucker ever go home?

"*Inglese,*" I demanded.

"Ee — " He cleared his throat. "Yes."

---

[5] Spoons. Sprinkling in foreign words feels like a cheap trick, but it seems to work for Michelle.

# Vaporetto

I held my phone in front of his face, Michelle's email open on the screen, and pushed past him toward the rickety elevator. I turned back after pressing the call button, baring my teeth. "*Vaffanculo,*" I said.

———

The room had one bed, a king-size, its foot facing the door, and in its exact middle slept Ethan, bundled in small blankets with his teddy bear. Michelle hugged me at the door then sat on the mattress, leaving me a small rustic chair in the corner.

"You're right, I can't just take him," she said, looking at the floor. "I'm sorry." She sighed. "I need your help."

The reading had been bumped up to tomorrow, and my name removed from the bill, and Award-Winning Canadian Author Michelle Melanson[6] needed a babysitter now that her novel was being released in Italian translation.

"I have to be there in the morning, for sound check," she said. "And there's the writers' workshop lunch, and I have to set out my books, and — "

"I'll take him for the day."

"Fine." Her expression relaxed. "Thank you."

I stood up and began walking toward the door.

"Where are you staying?" she asked.

My hesitation gave me away.

"You don't have a room, do you?"

"I tried," I said. "Thirteen hotels." I turned the knob. "It's getting late . . ."

She rolled her eyes and said, "You don't have to beg," lying back, left of Ethan. She pointed to the right pillow. It would be

---

[6] Alliteration sells.

like the weeks before he got his big-boy bed, when he had slept between us, just before Michelle began lying in his room with him until he dozed off. She had been getting up early with him in the mornings, too. She wrote while he took his daily nap. I never got the time she did, teaching every day and watching terrible student material creep into my work[7], drinking with the latest visiting writer or dallying with my workshop's newest heart-shaped ass then coming home drunk late, if at all.

At some point, Michelle had begun waking up in Ethan's bed, too.

———

We slept facing each other at the Giardino — at home, we turned our backs in — and we both awoke looking upon our sleeping son. I lay there until Ethan stuck a finger in my nose, chirping inquisitively, "Da-dee . . . ?", and when Michelle left she kissed me on the cheek: a simple peck and a whispered "Thank you" before her exaggerated Wave Bye-Bye with Ethan. He cried after the door shut and I considered doing the same, wanting to rage around the hotel room, to let my face turn red as I exploded, releasing it all. But there was something in the way her lips brushed my face: *I'm not finished with you yet.* Maybe she'd even forgive me. I was married when we met, for Chrissakes.

A sugary breakfast had been set out in our room the day before, plastic-wrapped Nutella croissants beside the coffee maker and one-serving sachets. In the small fridge, Michelle had left a half-bottle of orange juice, which I poured into Ethan's green cup. He sat on the bed in his overalls and smeared his mouth

---

[7] You know what I mean: stories about academics misbehaving, or dead babies, or things that too obviously actually happened to the writer, and with footnotes — always footnotes — because David Foster Wallace used them.

with the brown goo while cartoons pattered from the television. They were better when you couldn't understand them: dumb-shows about blind quests at deafening volume. I carried him to the bathroom and lifted him to the sink, where I washed his face and hands. We sang "You Are My Sunshine" while I slathered him in sunscreen, and when I squeezed a button of the repellent from the green tube, Ethan buzzed his lips and used a finger to trace a flight path. I finished and began buzzing, too, landing my bug on the tip of his nose. He pushed it away and giggled.

In the carless bustle outside, we met couples pushing strollers and wandering American-average families of four, all of them perplexed, as I was, about what to do with a child here. The glistening Doge's Palace was hopeless and, for Ethan, the most exciting part of a gondola ride — an eighty-euro gondola ride — would be the tippy steps in and out of the vessel. These were nothing compared to the wash and horns and rumbles of the *vaporetti*, the slow boat buses along the canal. The multi-coloured buildings would keep rolling into view, and we'd never stop long enough to smell the rot beneath.

———

I don't remember a splash, but there must have been a sound. He didn't scream or cry, and I didn't see his face. His head didn't bob above the water, not then and not anytime over the next three days, the seventy-two hours until the police stopped looking. The mustached officer, Giorgio, let me off his boat near the Piazzale Roma, the stop for buses from the mainland, when it was nearly midnight and the final search run was finished. Inside the station he tore up my swimming ticket and he handed me the sippy cup, recovered from the *vaporetto* floor. He showed me into his office, where Michelle had waited. Her chair was empty now. We had shared the Giardino bed for three more nights — not sleeping, not fighting, not even talking — and I had wondered if this would bind us together, if we would somehow emerge stronger; damaged, but stronger. But before the last search run, she had told me this was it: she was returning to Canada, and she'd be out of the house in three days and moved into her mother's. I wasn't to come home before then.

I thanked Giorgio and crossed the modern bridge, a bluish steel-and-glass ramp toward Santa Lucia, where just three days before I had dragged my jet-lagged ass off the train to save my marriage. A light rain began to fall, forming a mist over the water that was illuminated by the city across the canal — the stinking, foul-as-ever canal. I took the Scalzi and made my way back toward the Giardino, over infinite small bridges straddling infinite rivulets. At some point a gondola passed under me, carrying a hunched and wet forty-something couple, laughing as the pilot stroked double-time. I sat down and dangled my legs over the edge, watching the craft turn down a smaller channel, farther yet from the boat buses and the suction they created, the force that dragged the muck through the propellers. Giorgio had said Ethan had likely gone through the propellers. A mosquito began sucking my neck, but I didn't bother swatting. I just stared at the water. The rain fell harder, piercing the canal's surface, giving off more mist and a worse smell than ever. It dissipated into the night sky, and all I had made was gone[8].

---

[8] Thanks for taking a look, Bill. Be gentle, first thing I've written since. — R.

# Chaser
*for Nikita Nelin*

"*I* don't dream," Joana said.

Tom's bifocals rested low on his nose, under a brown-and-orange Browns cap. He inhaled while he thought. The tip of his cigarette glowed redder. "Some people say that," he said. "But did you ever?"

"I don't know," Joana said. "I don't think so." She reached in her once-white purse but came out empty-handed. Tom drew his pack from his denim jacket. He flipped the top open and she picked one, which he lit for her.

"Thanks," she said, and exhaled. She looked up at the sky.

Tom's Bar was the local in South-Collinwood, a narrow room in a crumbling ex-warehouse far enough from downtown to see stars. Joana was usually the only person here other than him, and if two die-hards hadn't stayed till last call tonight, they would have closed early. Now it was 3:00 AM, and she and he sat on the back step near the dumpster in the alley. It was this silence she loved most, listening for what Tom would say next.

"Everyone dreams," he said. "The question is more like, 'Do you remember them?'"

"Well then, I guess I don't *remember*." She smiled. "Nothing since I was called Yo-Ana."

Tom laughed a little. "I have one most nights," he said. "And when I don't, I feel lost the next day. Two or three nights, and I get scared I'll never have another." He dropped his butt and stepped on it. Then he lit a new one. "If I didn't dream, I think I'd go crazy."

"You're already nuts."

He clamped his lips on his smoke and mock-applauded. "You're getting better at this," he said.

She hadn't joked or flirted at first. She hadn't bummed smokes, either. "I'm quitting tomorrow," she said.

"Please don't," he said. "You just started. I can't run the place by myself. And everyone I know's already worked here."

Joana laughed. "Not the job, dummy. Smoking."

"Oh," he said. "Good luck. It's tough to quit anything."

She rested the heel of her hand against her forehead and let the cigarette's fragile chimney grow, its smoky smell contaminating her hair. She avoided Tom's eyes and looked instead at the garbage bag, tied off, beside them.

"What's the matter, kid?" he asked.

She lowered the hand and laughed. "You, you old bastard."

He was only fifty-five, though — and at thirty-three, she didn't feel far behind. Every year showed in small creases around her eyes and new greys in her long brown hair.

Tom said, "No, seriously," and leaned over. "What's going on?"

Slowly Joana shook her head. "I'm thinking about moving again."

"I knew it."

"I'm sorry," she said. "I get tired, is all."

"Everybody does," he said.

# Chaser

"Yeah." She nodded. "Yeah." She stubbed her cigarette on the ground and stood up on the wooden step. She lifted the black bag by its knot. "See you tomorrow," she said. "Thanks for the smoke."

"You got it," Tom said. She knew he'd be keeping his eyes on the backside of her jeans as she walked to the dumpster. With one arm, she hefted up the bag and shoved it over the edge. The bottles clattered inside.

———

If she took one only when she needed one, she'd have no problem with sleeping pills; the problem was that she always needed one. She would kid the college boy who stopped in for nightcaps — who was secretly proud to have grown up here — that if resuming the Cold War meant she'd get her six-to-eight, she'd be up for it. She hadn't slept since Gorbachev, and the smoking wasn't helping. The last one of the night always left her heart racing, and wired her eyes open. She could have gotten more tonight — the 7-Eleven on her corner never closed — but she had walked past, half forgetting and half meaning to, and had turned down the street to her square concrete building, which at twelve storeys was small compared to the one in Vilnius, where she had lived as a girl. She unlocked her apartment door and softly swung it open, nudging her cat, Petr, who scrambled off the mat. Ten years had passed since the snowy evening in Brooklyn when Vasili had slipped in through the back door of their rented house and opened his coat, letting the orange handful escape with a *mew*. He had since returned to Russia — at least, that's what he had told her he was doing — and now there was no brown brick and no approaching wedding, just Petr, sleeping near the door whether she was home or not. She was never sure whether he wanted to stop her from leaving, or whether he was trying to keep her away.

She reached in the kitchen cupboard above the sink, where she kept the sleeping pills and Aspirin and antacids. The last were essential when she drank; when she drank, she smoked too much. She needed more nicotine than she could stomach cigarettes, which meant she was addicted, she supposed. She removed the cap from the Dozaids and dropped a white pill into her hand. As she replaced the bottle, the cupboard door slipped from her hand and closed with a bang. Petr ran to the bedroom down the hall.

She swallowed the pill and, without removing her makeup or brushing her teeth, drowsily pursued the cat and lay down on the bed beside him.

———

She awoke late the next afternoon and rushed to Tom's. She enjoyed the walk but not the way she fiddled with the waist of her jeans and her shoulder strap and fished in her ragged purse for gum or cigarettes, of which she had neither. When she arrived, the bar was ordinary, which is to say empty. Were the place ever full she'd quit smoking, she was sure, but sitting out back with Tom listening for the door chime was a gift in blue plumes. It wasn't just the cigarettes — it was him.

Still, today, when he said, "Come on, kid, we're goin' for a smoke," she shook her head and told him to go alone. His expression fell.

"Shit, you were serious," he said.

———

"A whole day," she thought. "That wasn't so hard." But now, home at 3:00 AM, the not-smoking was making her tremble.

# Chaser

She reached above the sink for the Dozaids. The box of nicotine patches beside them was still unopened. She had packed and moved it a few times, and now she brushed off dust from Detroit or Philadelphia and read the warning label: *Side effects may include vivid dreams.* She scoffed and opened a drawer and took out a spoon, whose back end she slid under the flap. She lifted her shirt off over her head, and she peeled the backing from a patch. She affixed it to her shoulder. In her black bra and jeans, she stood looking in her bedroom mirror and imagined the tan circle as a bandaged wound. She stared another moment before she pulled on the long T-shirt that had once been Vasili's, though she tried not to think of it that way.

---

"I was in a forest," she told Tom the next night, when they were out on the step. He was smoking; she still wasn't. "It didn't look familiar — I don't get it. I've never lived in the country, just cities, and I don't think I've ever even *been* in a forest. But I was running. And I was completely out of breath. All I could see were trees, black in the distance, then green and so alive as I ran past. Branches swirled like they were trying to grab me. I was on this path and it was the only way out, and my chest hurt and I was crying but I had to keep running."

Tom leaned closer to listen. His ember reddened as he inhaled. He breathed out. "That's it?" he asked.

"*That's it?* My first dream in years, and that's what you say? Yeah, Tom. That's it."

"Sorry," he said. "It's really common, that's all. Falling, running away. They're on page one in my dream book."

"You have a dream book?"

"I have a few," he said. "Some to read, some to write in."

"So what's it mean?"

"Depends," Tom said. "Depends who was after you. Did you look back?"

"No, I didn't."

"Can't help you, then," he said.

She stood up and walked inside to run the dishwasher for the happy-hour glasses. They could lock up early if no one came before the machine finished, though part of her wished someone would, to keep her off the back step. Her fingernails were chewed to stubs. She lowered the front panel and scooped in the soap, reached for the START button.

The door chimed. "Shot a bourbon, whisky chaser!" a man roared.

"Coming!" She hurried from the kitchen and found a man she had never seen before staggering to the bar in layers of holey coats and a thick, unkempt beard. Mere alcohol couldn't make a face this red. This man had been outdoors for years.

"Shot a bourbon, whisky chaser!" he roared again.

"You got it," she said, glimpsing his feral eyes. State law prohibited serving someone this drunk, but refusing him was the worse idea. She filled two shot glasses, one with Beam and the other with cheap Canadian rye, and set them on the counter.

"F-Five dollars." She hadn't stammered since her first year of English lessons.

The man took the bourbon and raised it to his lips. He snapped back his head, exaggerating an "Ah" after he poured it down. She could smell the sweat and urine baked in his clothes. He'd be found one winter, maybe this one, frozen dead in a bus shelter. Someone always had been, everywhere she'd lived. The man smiled. His face relaxed, and she could see his eyes had once been kind. "Thanks," he said softly, and turned his head slightly to eye the second drink. "How much?"

"Five," she repeated.

He brought his fist down on the counter. His mouth curled into a snarl. "*How* much?"

She got out, "Don't worr — " before he lunged. She ducked behind the bar, telling herself silently to stay down, and glanced at the baseball bat below the cash register. She heard the man rise heavily from his seat.

"I thought we were friends!" he howled. His stool flew over her, shattering bottles and the mirror behind them.

Then Tom rammed the drunk. The men grappled on the floor a moment until the customer went limp.

"I'll leave," he groaned.

"You're fucking right, you will," Tom said.

Tom rose first, and then the drunk, who teetered toward the front door. Behind the bar, liquor trickled in a stained-glass waterfall and collected in the jagged shards scattered on the floor. Joana tiptoed over them to the phone beside the cash register. She dialled 911.

The man's second drink sat undisturbed on the bar.

"Wait," Tom called. "You forgot your whisky."

The man turned back, smiling again, that same warmth rising in his face. Tom pointed to a table by the front window. "Just sit there," he said. "I'll get it."

"Get one for yourself, too," the man slurred.

Joana watched Tom's quivering hands pick up an unbroken green bottle — gin, though what was inside didn't matter — and take a glass from under the counter. He paused to consider it, then removed the cap and poured. He walked slowly back to the table, one drink in each hand, sat across from the man and set down the whisky. He kept the gin for himself. "Drink up," he said, miming a toast.

The man snapped his head back and downed the whisky. Tom brought the gin to his lips and held it there. He stared at the drunk, who raised his eyebrows, puzzled. When the red-and-blue lights flashed outside, Tom put his glass back on the table.

———

It was 4:00 AM when they finished sweeping up, after the police had left. With the light dimmers turned as high as they went the bar was a beacon on St Clair. Joana waited on the back step while Tom locked up out front. He joined her and flicked off the breakers, clunking the bar into darkness. He turned the door's bolt and stowed his tinkling key ring in the pocket of his jacket. His hand re-emerged with a pack of Marlboros. He looked at her.

She sighed, and nodded. Her eyes welled up with tears.

"Don't worry," Tom said. "You can quit again tomorrow." He handed her a cigarette and she put it in her mouth. He lit it, then his own.

Joana sobbed once then breathed the smoke in, out. "You used to be a big drinker, didn't you?" she asked.

"The biggest," Tom said. "Got thrown out of so many bars, I opened my own."

She wiped her eyes. "How long's it been?"

"Eight years." He exhaled. "Eight years and two wives."

"Why do people do that? Order two drinks at once?"

"It's about knowing there's a next one."

"Thanks for saving me," she said.

"You knew where the bat was."

"I'd never have gotten there."

Tom put his arm around her shoulders. "It doesn't matter. It's done now."

"It's enough to give me nightmares," she said. "*Me.*"

Tom nodded. "I'd understand if you can't come back," he said. "I mean, what are you still doing here, anyway? There must be somewhere you'd rather be. Some dream you're following."

Joana shook her head. She looked up at the half moon and the stars. This was as dark as the sky was going to get, and soon it would begin to lighten with the dawn. "I think I'll stay a while," she said.

# Rocky Steps

*W*ithout the school trips, Crystal would be out of a job. Almost no one else came to the museum so early, and walking up the Franklin Parkway while commuters whizzed by, she met only the joggers who climbed the stairs, circled the museum, and descended the hill atop which stood the sand-coloured art museum, shaped like a square parenthesis. In front of the columns, she wedged her large frame between four jumping teenage boys. She muttered, "Watch it," when one jostled her. They kept their arms raised and continued leaping and landing on the inlaid footprints, throwing combination punches every time they touched down.

It was nine on the nose, a sunny weekday and warm for May, but the day's promise had already been dashed. In the backpack slung over one shoulder was the registered letter she had crammed in angrily after it was hand-delivered this morning. David was suing for custody — David and that bitch, Janice — on the grounds that a two-parent family would be better for Gregory than Crystal's house near South Street, which was missing two square tiles from the kitchen floor. She had bought the glue but hadn't gotten round to fixing them.

Past the shouting children she nodded to Robert, the retired Vietnam veteran who worked the grand doors. As always he smiled. She unclipped the velvet rope, sidestepped past, and replaced it behind her. She noticed the updated pamphlets, *Over 200,000 pieces* lettered on their covers, and plucked one from the rack for Gregory. "Haven't you already seen them all?" a man asked. He was a teacher, bearded, in a sweater vest, watching his charges flock to the coatroom. Crystal gave a faint smile and shook her head.

In the staff room she removed her jacket and smoothed down her uniform, powder-blue blouse over navy slacks. She pulled her wiry black hair into the bun she hated and before making her way to her post she checked herself in the bathroom mirror. Mr. Framingham — who *insisted* on being called Mr. Framingham — always reminded the guards that the grooming standard was strict because all day they would be standing among some of the world's finest art. Crystal saw the situation another way: wouldn't the exhibits make her invisible? She hoped so. She had long struggled with her weight and this was a fat day, when she truly hated her hips and her thighs and her breasts. She blamed the late-night sneak-outs for cheesesteaks, but her friend Shonda had said *nuhn-uh*, her weight was genetic.

She arrived in seventeenth-century Beijing and checked her watch. 9:07. Were he here, Mr. Framingham would have chewed her out. She was supposed to arrive for nine, meaning five to or earlier, in the event that a keen vandal beat her to Gallery 226 and tried to fell the house Wang Cheng'En built. Glancing side to side, she assured herself she was alone, then sat down on the wooden chair left of the doorway — placed to give a panorama of the installation — and sighed. Relaxed. She had learned not to bother looking at the time again after settling in; her shift ended when it ended, and following the ticking hands only dragged it out. Over time — two years now — she had come to appreciate the silence.

"Crystal, a word?"

She jumped a little. "Yes, Mr. Framingham?"

"Just checking," he said, behind a false smile. He carried a clipboard in front of his black suit, where he ticked off a list with an expensive silver pen. She wondered if he had marked her late or simply present. His footsteps echoed and faded into the next exhibits, and again she was left in silence. She wanted to rise and inspect the Crozier collection once more, sixteen hundred items from everywhere in the world, but if Mr. Framingham had said it once, he had said it a thousand times: looking at the pieces meant not looking at the guests or their wandering, grimy hands. She sank back into the chair and the silence and awaited the hushed roar of another school group, the inevitable nasal drone of the bird-like Charlene. Crystal watched her approach and fixated on the dirty blonde hair frizzing out of its tight ponytail. Charlene was whispering to the teacher in the sweater vest, helping herd the children into the centre of the room. She adjusted her oval glasses and shrilly ordered, "Quiet, everyone." Then sure enough: "Or I'll send Crystal after you."

*Condescending bitch.*

But as always, Crystal smiled and mimicked smacking a baton in her open hand.

The children stopped talking and Charlene began her usual spiel about the Ming Dynasty, and the kinds of people Duke Zhao would receive in this, his former palace. The spiel never changed.

Every day, Crystal liked to pick out a different element of the exhibit to peek at. When she could afford it, she bought Gregory used photo books about these cultures that predated their own country, be it the Chinese or even the only-slightly-older French, who had built the grand boulevards she and David would have seen on the honeymoon they never took. She read the books with her son, who had just turned seven, and insisted that he not watch TV or movies rated PG or higher without her present. There was just so much children shouldn't have to understand. Take Charlene: at this moment, she was telling the children Wang Cheng'En was a eunuch, and answering the usual question about the term with "assistant."

Crystal had once asked, "What if you just said 'assistant' from the start?"

"I don't tell you how to do your job," Charlene said.

"I just mean that they're kids. You've got to speak their language."

"These ones aren't like Gregory." She let the remark sink in. "These kids are from DC and New York and Boston. They've already been to Natural History, MoMA, the Smithsonian, and if they wind up in Philly instead of at Harvard or Yale or Princeton — even if they go to Penn — their parents will call them failures."

"You went to Penn," Crystal reminded her.

"I still do," she snapped. "And once I finish, I'm never coming back here."

No Master in Art History plans to be a tour guide, and no Law Enforcement Foundations graduate intends to be a contract security guard. Crystal had heard it before about Philly: New York's little brother, the capital before the new, better capital was built. But she would have preferred Penn — or Temple, Drexel, or St. Joe's, for that matter — to South Philadelphia

Community College, which began offering LEF when the city police department promised an increase in African-American officers.

No one had told Crystal there would be no bump for women. She had met David at South Philly CC before he passed his finals, before Gregory was born, before David joined the force and developed his thousand-yard stare and before she called his own unit on him one night when he came home drunk and threw the tiles for the new floor at her. David made more money than she did and, with Janice, he had recently bought a row house near the French Quarter where every second weekend was a free-for-all for Gregory. He ate nothing but cheeseburgers and played violent video games for hours.

"Why I gotta eat this?" he had barked when he returned from his last visit.

"Because it's healthy," Crystal said of the small portions of chicken, potatoes and broccoli. "You don't want to get fat like me."

"But if you eat it, how come you're fat?"

Her own mother would have slapped her smart mouth.

"Mama got started too late," was all she said.

"You should work out."

"You're right, I should," she said. "But I'm so tired after work. And we can't afford the gym. Even the Y costs money now."

"Rocky didn't need no gym," Gregory said.

"Didn't need *any* gym," she said. "And *Rocky*? Where did you see *Rocky*?"

The boy smiled. "Dad let me watch it."

"Well, I'll have to have a talk with — "

# Rocky Steps

"No, listen," he urged. "Rocky just ran every day. Every day he went to the museum and ran up those steps, and he got strong enough to beat Apollo Creed, the greatest fighter in the world."

"Honey, he lost to Apollo Creed."

"No, in the *second* one. He wins in *Rocky II*."

Crystal rolled her eyes.

"You go to the museum every day, Mama. Why don't you run up the steps?"

"Eat your broccoli," she said, rising from the table and taking her plate to the sink. The kitchen counter was littered with dishes. She plugged the drain and turned on the faucet. Gregory finished his meal and joined her to dry.

On the living room couch they looked through the Paris book together, comparing the Place de la Concorde to Logan Circle and the Hôtel de Crillon to the Free Library. They opened the art books, too, collections of paintings by Pollock and Johns that she had seen in the contemporary wing. Gregory's reaction to *Good Time Charley*, a grey canvas with a windshield-wiped arc made by a ruler that had then been pasted on with a paper cup dangling from its tip, summed up thousands of visitors' conversations: "Weird."

As Crystal tucked him in, he said, "In *Rocky IV*, Ivan Drago killed Apollo, but then Rocky beat *him*. Rocky said — "

"It's just a movie, honey. It's not real. I mean, didn't Rocky also get in shape by chopping wood and punching frozen meat?" she asked.

"Uh-huh, he did — and you forgot pulling the sled in the snow!"

He sat up and begged Crystal to take him to see the statue again, the one now at the bottom of the museum steps and well out of the postcard shot.

"We'll go on Saturday," she said, "but we have to go *inside*, too."

"Is there more stuff inside?" Gregory asked. "Like his gloves?"

"No, baby," Crystal said. "But there's lots of great stuff in there, like knights' armour, and paintings, and pottery — "

"Why do I want to see baby toilets?"

Crystal shook her head and pulled the blankets up to his chin.

—

The next weekend, as they walked along the Franklin, Crystal imagined the Champs-Élysées: more trees, fewer cars, the twinned smells of bread and cigarettes. "You know, this street was supposed to look just like the one in Paris," she began, but she stopped. Gregory was opening a gap ahead of her, and besides, she didn't know much more to say. They passed the Rodin Museum and then the bronze statue of George Washington surrounded by wildlife. Gregory charged up the museum stairs and Crystal followed slowly, watching as he jumped and yelled at the top, throwing flurries of punches and endangering abdomens all around him. When she finally reached the top she put an arm around his shoulders, supporting herself.

"All right, that's enough," she said.

"Can we go see him?" he asked.

"Okay, but remember our deal."

Gregory ran down again as she took in a deep breath. She held the railing and caught up to him beside the fighter, sculpted crudely with his gloves held high. They waited in line as groups of four, five, ten tourists took photos in front of the statue. When their turn came Gregory ran forward and raised his arms. "Come on, Mama!"

She tapped a Japanese man on the shoulder and handed him her cell phone before squeezing in behind Gregory. He still had his hands raised.

"Say *I can change!*" Gregory cried.

She said nothing.

"Come *on*," he begged.

Crystal lifted her arms. "I can change," she mumbled through a forced grin.

"Louder!" Gregory said. He smiled up at her, and she returned it.

"I — can — change!" they yelled together.

"Let's go inside!" Gregory screamed, running up the stairs again.

"Thank you," Crystal said to the man, looking a second at the photo before chasing after the boy. She ran the whole way. Above, Gregory had turned back to jump again, but he stopped near the summit. Still catching her breath, Crystal lifted her head and followed his gaze. City Hall's roof was a deeper blue than ever, and in the sun the newer glass buildings shone. She breathed in deeply, found the bottom of her lungs. This afternoon, she would fix the floor, Monday she would phone Community Legal Services, and in a moment they would enter the museum.

But right now, the skyline was beautiful.

# Gleaner

*B*righam's a small town like thousands of others — public and Catholic elementaries, a public high school the province tries to shut down every spring, hospital on the outskirts they built years ago, one dentist, one lawyer, and Robert Grand — Bob — the doctor who runs the little medical clinic.

Bob took some government money to practise out here — to be the one to tell farmers who never go to the doctor that yes, that thing in their guts is cancer, and no, it's too late, nothing can be done. He's from Toronto, and on the weekends when the clinic is closed and someone like me has to drive an hour to London when I drop a paving stone on my foot, he's on the 401 in his BMW, often with his hot, younger wife, leaving his three-storey red-brick mansion and five acres on the edge of town in the care of his landscaper, which is me. I'm almost forty-five and I've worked for him the last three summers, manicuring the grounds foot-by-foot, putting in koi ponds and wiring lighted pathways and doing whatever else might quiet Lisa Grand's "Get me out of this shithole" pleas for another year.

I can see why someone from Toronto wouldn't like Brigham, but I've lived here my whole life and I don't mind it. There's still a grocery store, and an arena with two well-kept ball fields behind it, and a little coffee shop you can sit in all day if you want to. It's where everyone reads the local paper, the *Gleaner*, which, I've got to admit, is a mystery. There's nothing to report, and the editor, Reg Small, is the whole of its full-time staff. The articles are basically ads — the minor hockey fundraising supper Friday, the scout troop car wash Saturday at the grocery store, the United Church's hundred-and-forty-seventh anniversary on Sunday — and I think they're all written by this year's high school co-op student, who will soon move away to study journalism and never look back.

So you can imagine my surprise when, taking my morning coffee break from the job at the Grands', I see a new quarter-page advice column.

Hi Hattie,

A few nights ago, I was out walking my dog, and across the street I saw a prominent local doctor strolling arm in arm with a much younger woman who isn't his wife. I'm anything but a gossip, but I have known the doctor's wife for a long time through church and community activities. I don't want to meddle in their marriage — or cause a stir based on a situation I might have misinterpreted — but I can't imagine it will be long before my friend gets wind of her husband's affair. What should I do?

— Burdened in Brigham

Mark Rogers' deep, scratchy voice interrupts from a table across the otherwise empty shop.

"Bobby Grand, huh? Gettin' a little on the side." He pushes his toothy smile through his fat, stubbly cheeks. "I know who with, too," he says, pointing a flabby wing toward the counter, where Miranda Knapp is flipping through a magazine.

In profile she's mostly black hair in a ponytail, an almost-too-big nose and a bony shoulder under the black strap of a bra her grey tank top doesn't cover. I watched her grow up — I've known her dad, Frank, since high school, a born mechanic — and since going to college she's come back to her old job at the coffee shop every summer, which makes me think that no matter what she's studying, she'll end up back here one day. She'll have her pick of men when she does, too, and I doubt it'll be just the single ones.

If I were Frank, I'd have never let her near the barn parties, where people get just as high and drunk as they did when they were eighteen, no matter how old they are, falling down and fucking up like they always have. But I guess after a certain age, you can't control your kids anymore. Miranda has come to resemble more than one farmer's daughter cliché, but home wrecker? I can't see it.

Of course I don't answer Mark. No one really does. He sits in the shop every day making comments about everything he sees, everything he overhears, and ends every sentence with half a question mark, hoping you'll toss him any scrap you have. I pick up my Styrofoam cup, still half full, and head for the door, dropping the paper atop the wooden trash bin. I stop and reach back for it. I haven't read Hattie's advice yet.

———

Bob Grand has a load of sod dropped off today — it's been a dry spring, his grass is still brown — and Duck Parker smirks when he steps down from the red cab and slams the heavy door that reads *Duck's Trucks* in white script.

"You read about this ol' dog this mornin'?" he asks, jabbing an elbow toward the house.

"Nah," I say. "Think I missed that."

"He's steppin' out on his wife," Duck says.

"Jesus," I say, probably too flatly to seem surprised.

Duck's smile widens, and I can barely see his eyes for his crinkling cheeks. He's got to be seventy now. "Makes me wonder," he says. "He ever leave her here when he takes off to the big smoke?"

"Would you really want anything to do with her?" I ask. Lisa's an educated, driven woman who almost won the last township council election against Shawna Myers, who's held the seat for years. She tried everything, said almost anything to knock Shawna down a peg. It occurs to me that Shawna might be *Burdened*. "Letter might be bullshit," I add.

"Fair enough," Duck says. He looks away for a second, looks back. "Well, sod's in the back." I help him lower the big tailgate and he's gone, leaving me to lay the squares of green on the dark earth I tilled yesterday.

—

I still go to the barn parties. They're always a little out of town, so everybody drinks and drives, but the cops have a handle on who they can trust to get themselves home. It's the teenagers you've got to worry about, the kids without the experience; we've all been doing this for years, but them, they end up with their picture in the *Gleaner* and their bodies buried in Brigham Municipal.

The few farms that regularly host are on gigantic lots with huge houses and a pool, plus fire pits and manicured horseshoe pitches or custom cornhole set-ups near big drive sheds where the food's laid out. It's always BYOB. The crowd's always the same people, and over time the sleeping kids you remember being eased into cars in the wee hours become legal to drink — become parents themselves. Frank and I still chirp at them to get out of their folks' liquor, regardless. Tonight, we're at Garrisons'. They always hire a band that plays half classic rock and half pop country junk. Like usual, there are ATVs and golf carts and John Deere Gators floating around, taking off down the path toward the bush most everyone has on the farthest reach of their property, where sometimes — like at Garrisons' — there's a cabin where the young ones fuck, or a clearing in the woods where you "go to see some stars," which is a shitty cover story for going to fuck. After a couple of hours, the teenagers take off to town for a stag and doe or to a London bar with siblings' old IDs, and us old folks just putter around for something to do, cruising from scene to scene like high rollers at mansions we've seen in movies.

It's still early, but I'll likely leave soon. I've already caught up with the usual suspects, the guys I've seen around town my entire life, and Frank has left for the dance at the arena. It's Thistle Days weekend, the annual bullshit Scottish festival — Brigham's clearly an English name — so a lot of people have gone and the party's dying out. I'm standing on the concrete pad behind the drive shed smoking a cigarette, thinking I should pack up my cooler and get home; Bob Grand has no problem working me Sundays, and nothing looks worse than a half-sodded lawn. I butt out and start to walk when a headlight swings around the side of the building. I jump back but the golf cart smashes into my knee.

"Sorry!"

It's Miranda.

It hurts, but not much. Max speed on these things is what, twenty?

"Are you all right?" she asks.

"Yeah." I grit my teeth a bit. "Ouch." It's dark but I can see her eyes are kind of wild. "You should be more careful," I say. "Too much to drink, maybe?"

"You sound like my dad."

"I know your dad." I smile a little. "He's a better guy than you think." It's not the first time I've told her this, not by a long shot; her teenage years weren't the easiest, with her mom dying and boys always at the door.

"He'd kill me if I drove home," she says.

"Move over."

She slides across the vinyl seat then leans her head drowsily against the roof support. I squeeze in behind the wheel and steer onto the long lane that goes from the bush all the way to the road. As we pass the front of the shed, the partygoers turn to watch us. Some start a slow clap, while a couple of jaws drop among the older ones.

"You sick fuck!" someone yells.

I stop the cart to get off, but Miranda grabs my arm. "I think I'm going to puke," she says, slurring a little. "Take me home."

"Okay." I move my foot from the brake to the gas. "Okay."

—

I wake up at 5:00 AM like usual, but with a headache and a foggy memory. I hit snooze and stay in bed.

Frank wasn't home when I dropped Miranda off, and the poor kid was so smashed that she fell into me trying to hug me on the way out. I caught her and as I held her there I realized it was the closest we had ever been. At her mom's funeral ten years before, I hadn't hugged her — or Frank, even. Since the car crash, he's been single like me, only I've been single . . . well, my whole life. I've heard some people think I'm gay or into some weird shit. But I just never met a girl I could open up to: a woman's touch, even a pat on the shoulder, has always sent me into a cold sweat and an uncomfortable tremble. Miranda's hug was like that, and I'm pretty sure now that I kissed her cheek before she got out of my truck.

Miranda is probably the most popular girl to come through Brigham, and not in that peaked-early, small-town-high-school way. She hated all the girl stuff, quitting volleyball and ignoring the students' council and ditching the prom to get drunk in a field. Prom night was a real blow-up with her dad. But she was never a puck bunny or a tough girl, either; just the good kid everyone looked out for after the horrible accident.

And now, I'm the guy who finally took advantage of her — or at least, that'll be the word around town. I can imagine next week's *Gleaner*:

Hi Hattie,
I recently saw something that absolutely mortified me: a man in his forties that I've known since high school left a large party with the drunk, barely twenty-two daughter of a man we've both known a long time. They looked pretty chummy, and a lot of people saw it, but her father wasn't there at the time. Should I be the one to break the news?
— Bowled Over at Barn Party

—

I won't tell Duck, but yeah, this is one of those weekends: Bob's away, Lisa's home. Over the three years, I haven't spoken to her much. Most days I just set to work, but today I don't get to the stack of sod before she calls me.

"Hi, Jason!" She's on the porch, wearing a pale green sundress.

"Want some coffee?"

I start up the flagstone path I laid last summer, and when I get to the stoop I poured two years ago, she stands up. She has bags under her eyes, like she's slept even less than me, and her blonde hair looks like it hasn't been brushed yet. She hands me a hot blue mug.

"Do you start this early every morning?"

"Yeah."

"I hadn't noticed." She tilts her head toward the empty chair beside her. "Sit with me a minute." She's quiet a few seconds, then takes a deep breath through her nose and says, "I'm just to going to ask." Rummaging under the *Star* and the *London Free Press* on the small table beside her, she pulls out the *Gleaner*. "Did you see this new advice column?"

"Yeah."

"Has Robert said anything to you?"

I shake my head.

"You wouldn't believe how many people have called me about this," she says. "I'd heard things about small towns before we moved here, but other than Shawna Myers, no one's really pried into our business before." She fixes her eyes on mine. "This is going to sound stupid, but . . . is there anything you know that might make you think Robert is . . . ?"

"Absolutely not." She smiles. I take a sip from the mug. It doesn't burn my mouth so I down the drink. "Better get started. Lots to do."

"Thank you, Jason, for talking to me."

"Sure thing."

I can't wait to grab the shovel from my truck, to get back down in the dirt.

———

Monday morning, 10:00 AM, I'm on my way to the coffee shop again. If I time it right, which I usually do, I'll catch Frank. We bump into each other here almost deliberately a couple of days a week. We've been doing it for as long as either of us remembers. The bell over the door rings when I walk in. At the counter, Miranda looks up. I'm already well into the life stage where hangovers last two days, but she looks like she could dash off a marathon and is even dressed like it, in yoga pants and a sports bra under a three-quarters-zipped purple jacket.

"I heard a rumour about you two," Mark Rogers' scratchy voice says from across the shop.

I shoot back, "Don't you ever leave?"

He laughs. "Find me a job as good as my last one and we'll talk."

I don't remember him ever having a job.

"What's Frank think about it all?" he continues.

"Shut up, Mark," Miranda says. "You know it's bullshit — you probably started the rumour, actually."

"I would never," he says, smiling like a four-year-old with a stolen cookie.

Miranda turns her attention to me. "Cream and sugar, right?"

I nod.

She turns her back and pours my coffee.

"How you feeling?" I ask.

"Fine."

"No consequences from Saturday?"

"I threw up in the morning."

"No." I lower my voice. "Your dad. Has he said anything?"

"What?"

"You know," I say. "You know it didn't mean anything. And he does, too, right?"

Her mouth hangs open a moment. "Ew. God. Was it like *that* for you, Jason?"

"No!" I say, too loudly. I feel my face going red. "Of course not. I saw you in diapers."

"Forget it," she says. "Just — stop being weird."

She pushes my coffee across the counter and I turn toward the door just in time to hear it ring.

"Fancy meeting you here," Frank says, grinning. It's what he says every time.

"Fancy that," I mumble. That's my thing that I say.

I dodge left to go past him but he catches my arm. "Doin' okay, man?"

"Yeah."

"The guys at the shop, they told me some weird shit."

"Oh God."

He turns just enough that Rogers can't see him smirk. "If I was poking a hot young piece of ass, I'd be careful where I showed my face." My chest tightens; my throat goes dry. Frank lowers his voice to a whisper. "Lisa Grand." He lets out a low whistle. "No wonder the good doctor's stepping out." He backhands me twice on the chest. "He can't keep up with the Jasonator."

"I — "

"Coffee's ready, Dad," Miranda says.

"Thanks, hun."

"Oh — and I appreciate you giving her a lift Saturday, too," he says.

"Of course." I let out a heavy breath. "Anytime." I glance at Miranda, who looks at Frank.

"Wait — " Frank cracks a smile. "Wait, wait — you thought I thought . . ." He starts to laugh. "Jason," he says, "Jason, Jason, Jason . . ."

I laugh too, and look again at Miranda. I think her small smile means she's embarrassed for me: her father's best friend is as clumsy with women as all the idiots in backwards ball caps who no doubt hit on her at the campus bar all the time.

"I'd kill you, though," Frank says, still laughing a little. He looks at Miranda. "I'd kill you both."

———

Wednesday comes and so does a new issue of the *Gleaner*. On my coffee break I take a table closer than usual to Rogers, so I can confront him about the *Hi Hattie* letter he no doubt wrote about me and Frank and Miranda. I open the paper to the back pages but don't find it. I start at the beginning again and flip one at a time until *Bye, Hattie* jumps out from above Reg's editorial, a long-winded apology.

Apparently, the column was offered to the *Gleaner* in a bundle of automated publishing services; had I ever picked it up off my truck seat and finished it, I'd have seen the "All Rights Reserved" message from Syndicated Media Inc. According to Reg, a computer program searches the text of the *Gleaner*'s archives then selects a relevant *Hattie*; the keyword that turned up most often was Brigham. He goes on to write that while some doctor in some Brigham is probably breaking his marriage vows, it is not Bob

# Gleaner

Grand, who is "nothing other than a pillar of our community." Then he admits that he didn't read *Hattie* before it ran. Hasn't read or edited the syndicated stuff in years. And at the end of the column, the noble bastard resigns. I drain my cup and head for the Grands'. No one's home and there's a *For Sale* sign on the lawn. The last of the sod is still waiting for me. I finish before lunch then leave. The medical clinic closes and I have to scrounge for piecework all summer. I take a winter job driving a sander-salter on the county roads. I stop at the coffee shop when it's open, which is less and less, but Rogers is still there most of the time, eavesdropping as he finishes one word search puzzle book after another now that there's no more *Gleaner*. Things go back to normal, otherwise, or maybe get a little better. Miranda smiles at me every time I walk in. She never will get out of here.

# The N

*S*teven — never Steve, anymore — had worked for the bank for four years, his first serious job out of university. Every December, his salary had climbed more than the token amount and, thanks to the annual bonus, he had paid down his student loans and bought an overpriced condo on Bay Street that, nevertheless, was sure to appreciate. He got his hair cut every five weeks exactly, and set up RRSPs and TFSAs and life insurance and three credit cards, one of them platinum — things that had seemed like fiction before he started university.

Steven didn't like to think about Steve, whose parents were both factory workers. Food had been taken from Steve's mouth by sudden layoffs, dragging workers' compensation cases, and strike votes. Steven had begun leaving Steve behind the moment he was given the green T-shirt everyone in his dorm received, when the upper-year volunteer had read directly from his student ID and written his full name across the shoulders without asking. He was Steven to the other students he met before they all drifted off to other friends. By Thanksgiving he came to believe they had seen through him: they had realized he was a townie who still lived at home, or had noticed his shitbox car, a beater on its last legs that he gassed up with evening shifts at Canadian Tire.

# The N

Rachel, his girlfriend since tenth grade, hadn't seemed to notice Steve becoming more Steven with every long-distance phone bill he reimbursed his parents for, every Christmas gift of increasing value, every all-night bus trip to visit her at McGill. She told him after graduation that for her he was and always would be "just Steve." Steven had worked his ass off to forget Steve.

—

Steven had heard his manager, Louis, had a tendency to "get real" in the pub at the base of the office tower two over from theirs, where he would take off his jacket and roll up his sleeves to expose the faded, misshapen tattoo of a Les Paul guitar with a fleur-de-lys body that covered most of one arm. Apparently, he'd pound beers and stagger out to the sidewalk to smoke tens of cigarettes — "the last two pleasures I won't deprive myself of" — and explain why he'd never get married a second time, or recount his early-eighties road-life with his teenage punk band.

Till now, Steven had avoided these episodes, allowing himself the odd after-work drink but leaving well before Louis was after-work drunk. He couldn't get away today, though. Louis was putting together a young investors' conference in Montreal, and had emailed Steven saying he would be a perfect face on the brand: someone successful and young, with whom the target customer would feel comfortable. Of course, Louis didn't want to discuss anything in a meeting room — he'd rather "have a chat," "shoot the shit," "keep it real." A little after five, they took the elevator down from their thirty-seventh-floor offices.

Once they had ordered a pitcher, Louis said, "I've got a good bullshit detector, so don't lie . . . Why do you still work here?"

Louis was talking to Steve; Steven let a little through.

"Everyone's got to eat."

"Nah, really," Louis said. "Do you even like this job?" He took a pull on his beer. "You only stick around after work if you absolutely have to, and nobody seems to know anything about you. Do you have a girlfriend or play sports or listen to music or . . . anything?"

"Sure," Steven said. But was he lying? He thought about his last few nights. They consisted mostly of picking away at work projects, or his financial plan. Always his financial plan. In the background he had music . . . what was it? Same as always, probably; the MP3s he'd hoarded in his first year of university. "I guess you could say I'm a Dave Matthews fan," he said.

"All right," Louis said. "This is a start. Steven, the Dave Matthews fan, from . . ."

"Waterloo."

Louis broke into a smile.

"Steve from Waterloo — Waterloo Steve, like an old rock 'n' roller!"

Steven shifted his eyes downward.

"I can call you Steve, can't I?"

"I prefer Steven," Steven said.

—

On a plane a month later, in first class, Steven was sipping his first scotch, ordered at Louis' insistence. It was two in the afternoon, and Montreal was barely an hour by air. Louis, into a third glass, had been talking non-stop since takeoff.

"And here's the thing — you ever hear about bands getting ripped off in Montreal? Their vans broken into, their gear stolen?"

# The N

Steven hadn't, but he nodded.

"It's because *every*body gets laid in Montreal, man: drivers, roadies, ticket-takers, bartenders." Louis took a big slug of whisky. "Security." He cast his eyes down. "That city's what killed us, man. We forgot where we came from." He was quiet a moment. "Band never did bounce back." Another silence followed, just for a second before he slapped Steven's leg. "The chicks, though! Even if you were the ugliest fuckin' guy. And let's say — just *hy*pothetically — that you were so fuckin' ugly you couldn't even score in Montreal." He started sounding almost wistful. "Well, then you'd just go to the ballet."

Deep down, Steve remembered this meant strip club.

"You know, you can touch them," Louis went on. His eyes lit up. "We should get Habs tickets — game tonight then hit the rippers."

"Don't we have dinner with the guy from the Montreal office?" Steven asked. "Philippe?"

"Fuck Philippe." Louis paused. "Fuck, Philippe . . . yeah, I guess we gotta do that."

———

Philippe left them after expensive steaks on Sherbrooke — after Louis had forced most of the conversation toward the Habs' game they were missing or which bars from the eighties were still open, despite Steven's numerous attempts to steer discussion back to the next morning's event. Steven needed to know: was there anything specific to young people in Montreal he should mention? Was he expected to use the French he'd tried to brush up on over the last month, the French he was still hopeless with?

# HAMBURGER

Louis started teasing him the moment they were alone. "You're all business, Steve, Jesus — I think you scared him off! Philippe and I, we hit the rippers every time I get to town. Speaking of which . . ."

Eventually, Steven agreed to go for one more drink — not at a strip club — and now they were headed toward Rue Ste-Catherine, maybe Crescent, scouting for a bar that wasn't too obviously for students; Steven might have passed, but Louis was almost fifty and starting to look it, pie-eyed with his shirt untucked, his tie so loose it was almost undone. They turned down Rue de la Montagne. They passed their hotel, the Vogue, and, to Steven's surprise, a breakfast place he recognized, one where he had eaten with Rachel.

Had she lived in this area? Might she still?

Steven crossed De Maisonneuve, not realizing for a few seconds that he was alone. He turned back. Louis had stopped outside the Vogue. Wanda's strip club was on the last corner, and he was sure he knew what was coming next. But Louis looked defeated: the prospect of sleep seemed to have flattened his single-minded determination of just minutes ago.

"I'm going to call it a night," Louis said.

Steve burst out, "Seriously?" and wondered aloud whether Louis would sneak back out without him later. He saw the breakfast restaurant over Louis' shoulder and said, "Okay, sure thing," pretending he wanted to turn in as well before lying, "Ah, damn — I just realized, I forgot my contact solution."

"I didn't know you wore contacts," Louis said, slurring a little.

"There's a Jean Coutu around the corner that'll be open," pointing vaguely in the direction they had come from.

"Thanks," Steven said. "See you in the morning."

# The N

"Good night," Louis said, leaning heavily into the revolving door's brass handle.

—

Steven thought he remembered Rachel's apartment having a dépanneur underneath, but it had been four years: any number of stores could have opened and closed in that time. Plus, Rachel used to change apartments every year. He thought a moment. He was at least certain it hadn't been over breakfast that she had given up on him; that had been over a fresh lemonade on Avenue du Parc, on the other side of Mont-Royal, after they had gone up and down the mountain in virtual silence, Rachel annoyed the whole time. She had started a lot of sentences — "I'm moving on . . . ", "The last four years have been so hard . . . ", "I don't know where life's going to take me . . . " — but hadn't finished any. He had eventually pulled it out of her, with an "Are you breaking up with me?" to which she nodded and whispered, "Yes."

He had been sure Rachel had cheated on him, and he'd caused a scene in the little café, berating her about it.

He blew money he didn't have on an expensive hotel that night, plus a bottle of fine whisky and an express train ticket home; he couldn't face the thought of another cheap bus ride — another twelve-hour overnight milk run in a seat impossible to sleep in — with nothing to think about but her. The next year, he had boarded a Caribbean cruise and almost picked up a hot resort worker, shaking Rachel's ghost for a while before coming home and starting to pinball from one woman to another — but now, here he was, a real adult, wandering the streets half-cut at eleven on a weeknight and staring down into deps, studying the apartments above them one-by-one.

He followed the east sidewalk as far north as Sherbrooke, beyond which the businesses gave way to houses in a steepening climb. He turned back and descended along the west side toward the hotel. He was sure this was the street. How do you forget a name as romantic as Rue de la Montagne?

How do you forget a name at all?

Nearly back to De Maisonneuve, he began stepping down a couple of stairs at each dep he came to. Climbing up from one with a white sign and blue letters felt familiar. From the sidewalk he looked up at the apartment door, its imposing dark wood.

This had to be it.

All that was left to do was climb the stairs and knock.

What would Rachel say when she saw him? He was a catch now, he knew, but somehow he had become a guy women brush off with a text after three dates at most.

Rachel had loved Steve. That she had stopped one day, well, that wasn't Steve's fault. Steve was a lovable guy. Steve could just knock on some other door. Tomorrow, when Louis introduced him, he'd say to the audience, "Call me Steve."

But for Steven, just hours from victory, this was the end.

*fine*

# Three Deaths of James Arthur Doole

## 1

I found out a few years ago, when I started volunteering at the Legion, that all I had to do to get my father's military records was print a government form off the internet and send it away. The package that came two months later contained no surprises: just copies of his registration, enlistment photo, death certificate, grave location, and the letters and telegrams sent to Mom regarding his plane going missing over Belgium, his body being found, his interment.

Since telling me of Jim Doole's existence when I was twelve, Mom liked to mention that he was buried in Holland — Amersfoort, which is the Netherlands, technically. And throughout my teenage years, so long as Wayne Baxter, the man I called Dad, wasn't around, she raised the spectre of my father, cold in the Dutch ground, when she got exasperated with me: when I got a bad report card, when I knocked out a tooth playing baseball. But all these years later — I'm close to retirement, now — she's begun entertaining a theory aloud that he didn't die, but learned Belgian ("or whatever they speak over there") and took up with another woman, started a separate family neither of us knew about.

# Three Deaths of James Arthur Doole

It struck me as a joke at first, but the more she said it, the more it seemed she actually believed it. I was starting to worry her mind was going. I saw her most Sundays, for an hour or two in the afternoon, but otherwise it was just her and the TV — no friends or activities, no church, no internet of course. She hardly had any books, had never bought anything she didn't absolutely need, and had always been a purger, running the house with military efficiency. I had asked countless times over the years if I could see any mementoes, even one photo of my father, but it wasn't until I told her I'd be sending away for all this info that she admitted that she'd burned all his effects, way back when I was a kid, on a day when she just got tired of hiding them from Wayne. She hadn't wanted him to think she was holding a candle.

I only started processing all this ten years ago, when Wayne's death clobbered me with a relentless shame: I couldn't accept that it felt less like losing a Dad than just a familiar face, like the corner pharmacist or my old school bus driver. In one of my weaker hours I let my wife, Linda, convince me to see a counselor, and he suggested that I go looking for that bond: that I borrow Linda's history books, talk to vets at the Legion, and learn about my father's death without Mom's feelings (or lack thereof) filtering them.

Mom seemed beyond reach, anyway. She had always been a master at changing the subject, at pretending she didn't remember. But I had to be sure: what if she really wasn't remembering things? Over the phone I offered to show her the package, but she just carried on with the alternate history as though I couldn't disprove it, saying time and again that the truth was "lost to time." I brought the envelope over without warning on my next visit and spilled its contents across the coffee table. The photo landed face-up on top — I arranged the papers in that order first — and his black-and-white face stared back at us with clear eyes under dark eyebrows and an Air Force cap: James Arthur Doole, twenty-two, clean-shaven and almost smiling.

"Yep, that's him," Mom said, as though to dismiss it. She sat there a minute on her floral-print couch, not saying anything more, then sniffed. She shuddered. "I think I'm getting a cold."

"And inside, Mom?" I asked. "Do you feel anything inside?"

She huffed. "It's too late. Best not to stir it up."

What she didn't understand was that I fully intended to stir it up. I was born when she was twenty, father already gone to Europe, and now I was on the cusp of leaving the GM dealership where I had worked all my life, the last twenty-three years as Service Manager. I had never been on a plane or outside North America and neither had Mom — at least, not since she was eight years old, riding a ferry over from Ireland.

Linda was ready to retire, too. A generation ago, her pension as a high school teacher might have been enough to keep us both going, but people live longer now. And though Mom was always saying that she could die any minute — she was eighty-five — she still was in perfect health. If we were going to get across the ocean, this was the time to do it.

From under the photo I picked up the burial information and showed her: the cemetery, the plot, the row, the grave.

"Linda and I are flying there this summer," I said. "We'd really like it if you came."

She practically threw me out of her house. It was exactly as I had expected.

—

# Three Deaths of James Arthur Doole

I spent the week at work wondering whether she would want to see me Sunday. It was usually me who called her every couple of days, not the other way around, but I decided to give her time; I probably needed some, too. And then, late Saturday night while Linda and I were reading in bed, the phone rang. I can't explain what happened over that week, whether six decades of mystery finally came to a head or whether she was just mad that I knew more about her lost love than she did, but she said she hadn't been sleeping — that most nights she'd lain awake thinking about my father and the war and Europe.

"Does this mean you'll come?" I asked.

"If it will make you leave me alone about it."

I hung up and looked at Linda.

"No way," she said.

I nodded. I could feel myself grinning.

"This is great," Linda said. "This is huge." She thought a moment then her eyes lit up. "We should take the whole family."

"We can't afford that," I said. It was a reflex. Mom and Wayne had taught me well.

"It'll be worth it. I mean, what have we saved for? The house is paid off, and we have my pension, and it's not like you don't get one, too. We'll earn it back in a year." She reached over and held my hand. "Think we could work one more?"

I knew she could, so I said that I could, too.

—

In the morning I called Lori. Her husband Craig picked up and mostly stammered into the phone. He had been promoted to foreman last year at Little's Slippers, the somehow-not-out-of-business-yet footwear factory, and since their kids had started school, Lori had been back at work on the line there. In the background I heard her say, "Give it to me." She sounded tired when she came on, but then, weekends do that to parents.

It was a surprisingly easy sale, though Lori didn't love that we were paying; she insisted on redirecting what she would have spent on two weeks of camp for Kayla to us, as well as what they had saved by not putting Spencer in hockey school. "He's finally figured out the Triple-A team is going to keep cutting him," she said.

"And Craig?" I asked.

"Well, it's a lot of money, *y'know,*" she said, lowering her voice to imitate him. "But he'll come."

I walked out to the backyard where Linda was weeding the garden.

"Lori's in," I said. "Craig and the kids, too."

"Just Garrett, then," Linda said. She raised her eyebrows. Just Garrett — Garrett who had moved to Toronto to be a writer, who never called home, let alone visited. I had stopped phoning him because he never seemed to answer, but Linda reached him once in a while.

"I don't know," I said. "He probably won't come."

As she always did, Linda said, "Let me handle him."

Damned if Garrett didn't sign on. Apparently the city was getting on his nerves lately, and — this was new — he had always been curious about war cemeteries. He said he could probably work the experience into a story sooner or later, which made sense — he had already been mining our family history for years without telling us. Generally, we played dumb and pretended the internet wasn't too good out here, that we didn't Google him and read his little stories online. At least he was up front this time.

# Three Deaths of James Arthur Doole

—

In the departures lounge at Pearson later that summer, still two hours before the flight, I nudged Linda and said, "Maybe not the best Christmas gifts." Kayla, who was eleven, was a mess of light brown hair hunched over a Nintendo while, beside her, Spencer was an older, square-topped shaved head texting furiously on his iPhone. Linda just said, "Imagine if they didn't have them." Books and magazines rested on our laps — I had saved up the last two issues of *War Stories Monthly* for this trip — but we were already bored, too. We hadn't really thought through travelling with someone Mom's age. For one thing, it meant arriving even earlier than the recommended three hours before the flight. It wasn't me or Linda driving the pace, though — we could barely keep up with Craig, decked out with clip-on this and zip-up that to store everything he owned on his person, scouting signs and practically drilling the kids: "Turn left," "Stop here," "Stay together!" When we were finally through security, the kids had taken back their electronics, retreated to seats, and disappeared into screens.

"Have they even said *hello* to Mom?" I asked Linda. "I mean, so many kids don't meet their *grand*parents, let alone the greats . . . and I never met my *father*, which is why we're even going . . ."

She gently squeezed my forearm. She didn't have to say it: I was forgetting that the trip wasn't just for me. I took a breath and looked over at Mom, dozing beside me. She had dressed in a lavender blazer and skirt set, the likes of which I hadn't seen on her in twenty years, and she had even put on makeup: a barely blue eyeshadow behind her nicer wire-rimmed glasses, chosen in place of the plastic-framed Coke bottles she wore around the house, and bright red lipstick that was almost overkill against her pale skin.

"You look lovely, Edna," Linda had said when we picked her up, and I had agreed. Mom had replied, "Thought I'd show the old boy what he's been missing." Who was this woman? She was nothing like the mother I had grown up with, the one always saying things like "Watch out" before my baseball games, when other kids' parents said "Have fun," or "Be careful" when Linda and I put the offer on our house, when other parents would have popped champagne. The dutifully RSVPing Mrs. Wayne Baxter had been replaced by Edna Doole — or maybe even Edna *Miller* of County Cork, who I had certainly never met.

The spring in her step tapered off before we got to the airport, however. Mom's interactions with the gate agents and security officers got terser, and in the lounge she sank into a seat and promptly conked out for an hour. Linda went to sit with Lori and Craig, across from the kids, and Garrett still hadn't turned up.

"How you doin', Mom?" I had stayed beside her.

She stirred and looked over, starting a little. "I'm okay." Her voice croaked with sleep. "Though I guess I don't believe this is happening." She scanned the lounge and lowered her voice, as though afraid someone would overhear. "For so many years it felt wrong to even think about. And what's worse is I don't think Wayne ever said it was — I just shut it off by myself."

She seemed lucid, if not quite awake, so I tried: "You must have talked a little about it, though . . . ?"

"Well," she paused. "There wasn't much to say."

"I guess not."

"It all happened so fast, Paul. Your father was here, then he was gone — first to Winnipeg, for training, then before I knew it, for good." She took in a bigger and slightly shaky breath. "More than two years had passed by the time I got the telegram saying he was missing. And just a few weeks after that, the war was over and everyone was so happy. Every night was another celebration for someone else's husband or brother or son who had come home. I went to all of them — I took you, too — and sat on the edges of rooms where everyone else was dancing, wishing I could feel what they felt. And then when Wayne — he was your father's friend, they enlisted together — when he walked in, he came over, ghosts in his eyes, and put his arms around me. His mother was throwing this party, she was so happy to see him, and he didn't say a word to her — "

I put my hand on her shoulder.

"It all happened so fast," she said again.

"I can't imagine."

She looked up at the screen. "Brussels?" she asked. "I thought were going to Holland."

There it was: the classic Edna Baxter subject change. But a bit of story had slipped out this time.

"Flights were cheaper, Mom. And the train's only a bit longer from there."

Now if only I could get her to say, "Netherlands."

"And where's that Garrett?" she asked.

I checked my watch. He was cutting it close: you were supposed to be through security ninety minutes before takeoff. We were into the final hour. A few people were already standing and milling around the gate. The boarding call began and, finally, my son strolled up, his scraggly goatee longer and narrower than ever and some kind of crochet hippie hat over his hair — which had grown almost to his shoulders. He raised his hand in a cool-guy wave, not moving it and barely looking at me. When our eyes met he lowered the arm. He grabbed me in a hug, which was new, too. I gave it back stiffly.

"Did you lose your razor?" I asked.

He half-smiled. "I'll go with 'yes' this time."

"You look like you're homeless."

"It's — nah, forget it," he said, turning away.

Kayla and Spencer were beelining toward us. Garrett snatched the girl up, and in his monster roar there was a hint of an old man groan. She'd have been smaller and easier to lift last time he'd seen her, however long ago that had been; he'd spent recent Christmases with bands of yogis or surfers in far-flung places, and was working in an organic grocery store or something. I wondered if those little websites he wrote for paid well. It all helped the prodigal son act, though: Linda interrupted the man-boy-to-boy-man handshake with Spencer and wrapped Garrett in her arms, squeezing tightly until he coaxed her into letting go.

———

I had always passed right out on trains and buses, and it turned out that an airplane was no different. An overnight flight had seemed inconvenient at first, but after falling asleep before the flight attendant had even cleared my dinner tray, I woke in Europe with six hours of sleep under my belt and found morning already beginning.

"Never do," Garrett said, holding up his passport, metallic-embossed coat of arms and CANADA glinting. "It's the golden ticket — after what we did in the war, they worship us over here."

"We?" I said, shaking my head. He hadn't done anything, and neither had I.

# Three Deaths of James Arthur Doole

"What's that, Dad?"

"Nothing."

I was pretty sure he had heard me, but he zeroed in on a good spot beside the baggage carousel and walked off. After the suitcases came we wove our way through the airport toward the train platform, where the morning air was cool. The red engine with the sleek, too-long nose glided to a stop. Mom was napping again, on a bench. I gently shook her shoulder and we all boarded, occupying eight red-backed seats, four on each side of the aisle. Garrett sat with Linda, no doubt to regale her with adventure stories before telling her he needed money. Just like a writer. I sat with Mom and gave her the window.

I struggled to stay awake, in case she needed anything, but she didn't; she just looked through the glass, her usually neutral mouth hinting at a smile. The sky was brightening. I gazed across her at hayfields and pastures dotted with cattle or sheep and thought it looked a lot like home, where I hadn't often taken the train. I had forgotten how entrancing scenery could be sliding alongside me instead of head-on over asphalt and a dotted line. We transferred onto the yellow-and-navy Dutch train at the bright blue temporary station in Rotterdam — the main one was being rebuilt, we had no idea. Across from Kayla and Spencer, Mom and I took seats that faced toward the back of the car. Watching the place you were disappear — now that makes you feel like you're getting somewhere.

———

Inevitably the kids got into an elbowing competition over an armrest. I snapped my fingers and pointed a thumb toward their grandmother, now asleep beside me. It was me who wound up waking her, though, when the announcement came on in Dutch, then in German, then English. We had to get off in Gouda. Two trains had left Rotterdam at the same time, and I had led us onto the wrong one. I woke Mom, then Lori and Craig, then Linda. Beside her, Garrett looked up from a falling-apart paperback — a war novel, I think. I huddled everyone to the door.

Garrett checked the schedule on his phone. "We have eleven minutes," he said. He looked at Mom, then back at me, smugly.

We sent Lori and Craig and the kids to find the platform, Linda and me helping Mom move as fast as she could. Garrett took her bag ahead, looking back and urging us on. We rejoined the rest of the family frozen at the departures board. With no reason, or at least none given in English, the regional to Amersfoort had been cancelled. The next one was only thirty minutes from now, but I knew I would feel each of the eighteen hundred seconds.

Garrett looked toward Kayla and Spencer and said, "Nice one, Grandpa." The kids didn't even try to hide their smiles.

"I didn't see you helping, Mister World Traveller!" I exploded. "You're so smart, you could have told me!"

He pushed a *ffft* through his teeth and said, "Whatever."

"That's everything with you, isn't it? *Whatever.* Why are you even here?"

"You asked me to come."

"*I* didn't invite you — "

I felt Linda's hand on my arm. She looked at me and then at Garrett.

"Don't forget who you're here *for*," she said, sternly but softly, trying to get below Mom's hearing threshold. "You will not do this here, or anywhere on this continent."

Garrett nodded.

Linda fixed her eyes on me.

I said, "Got to come out sometime."

"Not here," she repeated.

I nodded, too. Garrett turned away from us and adjusted his backpack on his shoulder. His book was still in his other hand and, after walking down the platform a short distance, he took a seat and resumed reading. Linda went the other direction and joined Lori and Craig, leaving me standing alone. It would've been a perfect time to get back to *War Stories Monthly*, but right now I just wasn't interested.

———

I let out a heavy breath and looked up at the screen. Sixteen minutes. I watched it till the first digit disappeared. Nine became eight then seven, six, five; an announcement, squealing brakes and air releasing, a cluster of indistinguishable voices as people got off and we got on, then the first slow chug, the slightly faster next one, and the accelerating sound of us leaving the station.

I hadn't noticed where I had sat down.

"Uh, Paul?" Craig was beside me. "Linda's got your mom, and Lori says she's going to sit with Garrett. They think you and I should talk the rest of the way."

I said, "Sure," instead of the *Whatever* that came to mind. The half-smile on Craig's face suggested he found this as contrived as I did. "And what do we talk about?" I asked.

"Our boys, apparently."

"You were given a topic?"

He laughed and said, "*Your* wife did that."

I smiled and walked through the most obvious in-door. "Linda said something about Spencer not playing hockey this year?"

"Yeah," Craig said. "All of a sudden it's too fast for him out there — and some of the kids have gotten way bigger. It's actually dangerous."

"We just told Garrett to keep his head up."

"And look where it got you guys."

"Yeah," I admitted. "I pushed Garrett pretty hard. But he was quitting everything then, and smoking dope, too, I think." I pursed my lips but a big breath got through. "We didn't know all we know now about concussions . . . "

"My old man pushed me, too," Craig said. "And I hear yours was no softie."

"Mom had a thing for military men." I smiled at the poor dummy. In the seat pocket in front of him was his blue Netherlands travel guide. "Gouda," I said. "What's your book say about that place?"

He laughed. "Just the cheese market." He leaned into the aisle and looked at the kids, noses still in their gadgets. "Can you imagine trying to interest those two in a cheese market?"

I laughed too.

"Of course," he added, "if me or Lori are involved, they aren't interested in *anything*."

"Garrett was like that, too," I said. "Just started pushing us away one day." I thought a minute. "I probably did the same to Wayne."

"You don't get much time," Craig said. "And you notice right away when they're across that line and they'll never be your little kids again. Of course, those two have always been like little adults, negotiating everything . . . "

"But you talk."

"Yeah," Craig said. "We do."

# Three Deaths of James Arthur Doole

—

The train lurched a little and began to slow. I was starting to think stations all looked the same, but once we were off the platform and out to the taxi stand, I turned back and gawked at the tall glass façade and the pair of two-storey burgundy bowls on pillars sticking out of its front. It looked like someone had cut a boat into halves and stuck them there.

"Got to be Gary," Garrett said, pulling his phone from his pocket and thumbing buttons. A minute later, he muttered, "Huh, maybe not." He was good with that thing; he had looked up all the info on baggage lockers so we could head right to the cemetery, before even checking in at the hotel — to everyone's surprise, that's what Mom wanted.

"You don't want to rest?" I had asked. "Or go tomorrow?"

She had lifted her head higher than I'd seen in years. "If I go to sleep now, after coming so far," she said, holding back a laugh, "I might never wake up."

Lori had said, "Oh, Gram."

We split into two cabs, by gender. I looked at Craig then braved a conversation with my son. "Who's Gary?"

He turned back a little in the front seat. Of course he had taken the front seat. "Frank Gary." He guessed from my silence that I didn't know him. "G-e-h-r-y. The architect. He redid the AGO."

"Oh, yeah . . ."

"The Art Gallery of Ontario."

"Right," I said. "Right. Had a field trip there in school. Of course I didn't go."

Garrett smiled. "Not everything's on the History Channel."

"You make it sound like I've never been to a museum," I said. "Just last summer I went to the Canadian War Museum in Ottawa — and at the Warplane Heritage Museum in Hamilton they have a Lancaster like the one my father flew."

"Huh," Garrett said. "Cool."

Craig looked up from his guide. "It's two and a half kilometres to the cemetery," he said. "Two and a half the other way, we'd be at a concentration camp."

"Great, Dad," Spencer said flatly from the middle seat. "Thanks for that."

Garrett laughed; Craig and I shared a glance over the boy's head.

—

The low-rise downtown gave way to houses, then the greener fringe of the city before our cab stopped at a brick monolith beautified with a small square of grass and lone cannon on two big wheels. The girls' cab pulled up behind and Linda helped Mom out. The eight of us approached the attendant's booth and I handed him the small paper on which I'd noted the grave coordinates. Flanked by tall pines' naked trunks and shaded under their canopy, we headed to the back where the war graves were; other than these four hundred, the rest were civilians. The website had said Dad was in the nicest section, but it was second best to the Soviet Field of Glory, which lay behind an ornate brick gate.

It felt rude to take such a direct path, efficiently ignoring the others on the way to this marker. There are cemeteries with more, but still, there seemed to be countless identical headstones, white crosses engraved with rank, name, serial number, nationality and a religious symbol, usually a crucifix though there was

an occasional Star of David or a blank space. I reached the plot
of seven men and leaned down and read the inscription. I called
out, "He's over here!" but no one responded. I looked back and
realized I had gotten ahead. "We found him, Mom," I said, tears
running down my cheeks.

Lori and Craig and the kids caught up first, then stood aside
so Mom could approach. I reached out and took her arm, pulled
her close to me.

"Shh," Mom said, hugging me back. "Shh."

2

I didn't react like Paul, either in Holland or when the telegram
came in 1945. In fact, as I hugged him back, I was embarrassed
for him, blubbering like a fool in front of all of us. But I understood, to an extent — his whole life, he's carried his father as an
idea, a war hero, the supreme sacrifice and all that. It probably
wasn't till he found the grave that Paul thought of an actual man.

I knew the actual man, though, and even before he left home I
was sure that if Jim Doole died, absolutely nothing would change
for me. Jim Doole not coming home would have been no surprise
at all. Of course I could never tell Paul that. Clearly he's got a
story that makes sense, and ends with him — and I think, in his
mind, me, too — accepting that our family was broken and has
never healed.

But I don't buy it.

It's after ten at night now and I should be sleeping, but I feel
like I've finally got it all straight. My legs hurt when my feet touch

the floor beside the bed. The window facing the desk is drafty. I take up the hotel pen and the complementary notepad.

—

Jim and I met in the summer — 1942, it would have been — when I was working in the munitions plant and he was at the foundry. We met at a dance at the Odd Fellows hall when he was fresh from six weeks of training, wearing his uniform like the ten or so other men he was with. He had been among the first drafted for the reserves on Home Defence. What I noticed most about him was his grey eyes, the sharpness in them. When he trained his attention on me, I was afraid to look away. He was serious; he seemed smart, and maybe a little dangerous. He was also drunk on whisky. I could smell it the first time he asked me to dance, and I'd smell it on him from then on. But he was kind that night. When he asked after just two songs if I'd like to go somewhere else with him — "anywhere else," he almost pleaded — I said I would.

We walked down Main Street to Viscount Park and sat on a bench beside the tennis courts. He held my hand and promised his intentions were entirely honourable — in those actual words — and said he'd like to marry me. But he was drunk, of course.

Paul, of course, needs to believe that Jim volunteered to die for his country — which, yes, he eventually did — but the thing was, he was happy with Home Defence. Well, not happy. He had a weight on his shoulders. The last thing he wanted to do was go fight. He went to train with the other men each time he was called, but not long after we were married he got tired of being called a no-good "zombie" by the volunteer soldiers, the newspapers, pretty much everyone who thought it shouldn't be just volunteers but also the drafted men going overseas. And that's when he really started to drink.

In the beginning, he was Sweet Jim when he'd had a few; six months later, he was nothing but a hard crust. I felt like I had been duped, like he'd put the whole act on so he could get married, so he could get me into bed but keep his conscience clean in case he did wind up killed in the war. He began coming home at all hours of the night, belligerent or just stupid, sometimes demanding my attention and sometimes barely making it to the living room couch before collapsing, waking up stinking and failing to show up for work the next day. It amazes me that he didn't get fired. At the time I guess they couldn't afford to lose anyone.

It was through Home Defense that Jim knew Wayne. I didn't know much about their friendship other than that, but since they had met, Jim wasn't coming home as late, or quite as drunk, or alone. Wayne helped him in, and came back in the mornings to make sure he went to work. In some ways, Wayne was a better wife than I was, though on the other hand, I think people call this "enabling" now.

—

I've heard it said that men get married hoping a woman never changes, while women always think they'll be able to change a man. I did think that getting married would settle Jim down a little, but every night when he came home he followed the same program: he started out sad or angry (sometimes both), then moved to sorry, then got insistently amorous, refusing to hear that maybe this wasn't the best night — or that maybe, just once, I wanted to make it to morning without someone crashing through the door in the wee hours. I hoped our first child would do the trick but I couldn't have been more wrong. When I told him I was pregnant the next January, his grey eyes narrowed and he just grunted, "Great."

He could be truly mean, and I never forgave him for that. I never learned to predict what would turn his look to lightning. His fury couldn't have been about just the war . . . he hadn't even experienced the war yet! And while our baby should have been a stepping stone for him, one more reason to avoid going over, of all the things he could have done, he used it as an excuse to go missing for almost two days. Around dinnertime the second day, he showed up stone-cold sober with Wayne at his side.

He fixed the eyes on me. "We enlisted," he said. "Air Force."

Those eyes. My knees went weak; the blood seemed to drain from my head and I had to sit down. I had been morning-sick all month. I felt the first tears.

"Why, Jim? Why would you do that?"

"Right thing to do."

It was so matter-of-fact: firm, final, non-negotiable. But I asked anyway. "Right thing for who?"

"Wayne and I are going to the mess now."

I looked at Wayne, but he offered no explanation. In fact, he said nothing at all. Why was he even there? Could Jim only muster the courage with him in tow? "Of course you are," was all I said.

As far as I was concerned, Sweet Jim died when our apartment door closed behind his meaner alter-ego. But wouldn't you know it, he was resurrected by two in the morning when, without Wayne, he came home subdued, reeking of whisky, and got into bed. He wrapped his arms around me from behind.

# Three Deaths of James Arthur Doole

"I'm so sorry," he said. I felt his tears on the nape of my neck and wriggled away, but he persisted. "I'll write," he said, "And I'm going to come home different. You'll see. This will set me right. We've got to be in or out, none of this halfway stuff. We need this war to end — and the only way is to win it."

This wasn't Jim anymore, but some conflation of ads and training-camp banter and the editorials in which men were constantly criticized for not doing what the authors would be last to sign up for. I might have fought him on it had we had the conversation in the afternoon, or anytime when he was sober; I might have reminded him he never wanted this war, but I knew he was gone. He was far from the first to cave after enough zombie duty. All we could have done that night was have yet another nasty argument in bed. I didn't know what he was doing in the morning — I didn't much care — but I had to work, which meant that right now I had to sleep. I said, "Whatever you say," and closed my eyes until finally I went under, long after Jim had started snoring.

There was a parade to see off the latest volunteers. The town wasn't very big, but every couple of weeks we seemed to march out another twenty men. I thought hard about not going; I still didn't approve of Jim enlisting, and though he'd wasted a lot of breath trying to convince me, I knew that deep down he was trying harder to convince himself. I knew I'd be fine without him — I have been, all these years — but the baby . . . I couldn't help but think it horrible that a child should grow up without a father.

I spent a lot of time talking to my mother before Jim left for the Air Force training school in Saskatoon. She insisted that I wait for him.

"Once he gets overseas," she said, "longing to hold his child might be what gets him home."

It was sentimental, but it struck right in the place Sweet Jim used to hit me, before he started just hitting me. You didn't get divorced back then, though. It was a big bet, and maybe a foolish one, that Jim's heart would win out in the end, but I put down everything I had. I wrote him every week about how I was feeling, about the factory, about anything and everything and, I'm sure I'd realize if I had the letters to reread, about nothing at all.

I didn't get one reply from Saskatoon, and he didn't come home again; I didn't know whether he had shipped out, or how long he'd be gone, anything. At the time, everyone was saying, "No news is good news." I came to believe it after a while, though probably not in the same sense that they did.

———

My letter-writing slowed over the next year. I worked as long as I could at the factory, gave birth, and was back to work again in about a month — so many women were working that the government had set up childcare. I missed that after the war. Paul spent a lot of time with his grandmother, my mother who had never worked a day in her life. I sent a picture of him to Saskatoon as well as letters that were probably more emotional than Jim would have wanted, some of them in Paul's baby voice, saying things like "I can't wait to meet you, Daddy!" Of course nothing came back. Nothing, until a postcard, maybe two months before the telegram: *In England*, it said. *All well*. No "love," no mention of Paul, no suggestion that he had received any of my mailings or even meant to send his own — and of course, no indication that he might ever come home. I imagined Wayne standing over drunken Jim and forcing him to write something, maybe even snatching the card away and mailing it before Jim could change his mind. Of course, Wayne wouldn't have been there — he didn't have Jim's eyesight, he wound up in the infantry — but cleaning up Jim's mess would have been just like him. It's what he did the rest of his life.

—

And then, the missing-in-action telegram. Paul was barely a year and a half old, but the moment had to have impressed on his brain. He was in the playpen, in the dining room, out of sight but within earshot. I was in the kitchen washing a sink full of plates and bowls — I'd had my mother and sister over the night before the message came. "Regret to advise you that your husband . . . is reported missing after air operations overseas . . . "

I wasn't sad to get the news. I was angry. He had left me high and dry, the bastard, and had known he was doing it. I crumpled the paper and threw it in the fireplace, never wanting to see it again, but it wasn't the last word about Jim. In the next weeks there was a letter from the squadron commander trotting out canned lines about Jim serving admirably and being well-liked by his peers — a pleasure to have in his ranks, a true loss to our country — and then the official letter from Air Force Headquarters in Ottawa. Then another telegram: "Regret to advise International Red Cross quoting German information states your husband . . . lost his life . . . " Letters came after that from the squadron chaplain, government ministers, politicians, and all kinds of other offices, all the way up to the king. It seemed that every time I thought I could get on with my life, someone else was sending something with "regret" in the first couple of lines. And the famous Last Letter that every bomber crewmember wrote before every mission? It never came.

I had regret, too, one great big one: that I had ever met James Arthur Doole.

But like I said, I was washing dishes, and after watching that little paper burn I got right back to the cold dishwater. I washed one of the plates, looked it over on its way to the drying rack, then slammed it down beside the sink. The way it shattered felt good. I grabbed the next one and the next and smashed every dish, and when I was through I put my hands back in the water. I had cut myself. The blood snaked out from my finger and puffed as it mixed with the soap. And then I heard Paul crying. I didn't know how long ago he had started. I stood there a long time, wondering whether he or the bleeding would stop first. He was still wailing a few minutes later. I took my hands from the sink and wrapped the finger in a towel. I lifted him out of the playpen with one hand and held him close to me. "It's okay, now, it's okay." If I said it once, I said it a hundred times. Paul and I had been okay on our own this long; I had been better, even. His gasps were hot on my neck but he was calming down. We went silent a moment. I looked up to the ceiling and thought, *Good riddance*, but for the two of us, I said only, "Goodbye."

Until this afternoon, when Paul was bawling in my arms again, I hadn't realized he had to say it himself.

—

# Three Deaths of James Arthur Doole

I check the little card Paul left me, with everyone's room numbers and extensions in case I need anything. It's after midnight, and today is just the beginning; we've still got a week of museums and canals and castles to see, Amsterdam and Bruges and Brussels, before we fly back. My fingers hurt from gripping this pen so long, and I really should sleep. But I don't think the writing is enough.

I dial Garrett's number.

"Yeah?" he answers.

"Did I wake you?"

"No," he says. "I'm working on something." I hear him take a drink. "You all right, Gram? You need anything?"

"I have something I want to give you," I say. "Will you come over?"

"In a few minutes?"

"Really soon," I say. "Don't let me change my mind."

"Two," Garrett says.

I sit on the bed and hold the notepad in my lap while I wait. There's a soft knock and I let him in.

He sits down beside me. "Why you up so late, Gram?"

"Different bed," I say. "Can't sleep. Also, I'm thinking a lot."

He pushes some of his long hair behind his ear. "Heavy stuff, right?"

I offer the hotel pad. "I wrote a bunch of things down, and I think I want you to have them."

Garrett takes the notepad. "What is it? A story?"

"The ramblings of a madwoman," I say. "Some things I've been thinking about for a long time — since the war, I guess. Some things I've never told your father."

"Nothing he hasn't already seen on History Channel, I hope."

From his smile, I can't tell if he's kidding. I want to take the notepad back already. What if he throws it in Paul's face, just to hurt him?

It's done now, though.

"I hope you get something from it," I eventually say.

Garrett slowly nods. "Thanks, Gram." He looks through the pages. "Should I read it now . . . ?"

"No," I say. "Take it with you."

# 3

*War Stories Monthly*

Going Down
by Garrett Baxter

Every day was fear. Every night was terror. Joe Moore thanked the lord every time he made it home; after that he drank with his crew till all hours, then awoke jittery and began chain smoking again, waiting for next orders. Everyone knew the average for a Lancaster was less than eight missions. Nine and up, you were borrowing dead men's time, and eventually, your credit would run out.

He had heard it used to be worse, though. At the war's beginning, bombing runs were daylight operations in smaller planes that couldn't take the abuse. The Germans had easily swatted them down. But now, the good guys had the Lancs, and in forty-three they'd burned Hamburg to the ground. "Black Mike" McEwen had taken over Six Group, on the Canadian side, and cracked down on the bedraggled way aircrew dressed, what he called "the fifty-mission look." He was an OC who flew with his men, and had become something of a good luck charm — not *fifty missions* good, that was just an expression, but already Joe's crew had sixteen painted lipstick kisses on Naughty Nellie's nose.

Nellie was named after a barmaid at the mess, where tonight Joe sat with the diehard lads. A crew ate together and bunked together, lived together and, too often, died together. Above all, it drank together, but tonight Mario "Frenchy" Savage, the navigator, and flight engineer Al "Boss" Hickey had turned in early. There'd be orders soon. Mick Easton, the wireless operator, and the unflappable gunners Bill Clark, mid-upper, and Don Patterson, tail, had followed one beer later. The dispersal had soured Joe's mood, and now just he and his bomb-aimer James "Clint" McClintock remained at their usual table, surrounded by a field of empty glasses.

"What I'm saying," Joe insisted, "is that Harris is the best chief Bomber Command's ever had. We'll keep running these missions."

"But we aren't hitting the targets! We're just dropping more bombs. Remember Dicky Mathers, before he went down? He said in the first two years they were missing everything by miles — really, miles! Remember how he used to say he had the record for most cows killed by an airman?" Clint drained the last of his pint. "Killed a ton of people for nothing in Dresden, too."

"Not for nothing," Joe said. "We're breaking them."

"Harris just wants revenge." Clint looked away. "But it isn't the people down there who bombed England."

The sign over the mess' hearth read *No religion, no politics.* Theirs was not to reason why, but maybe Clint had a point. After the success at Hamburg, Harris had attacked Berlin and Nuremberg but, scared by the Allies' coup, the enemy had shifted ten thousand anti-aircraft guns to home defense, and its technology had caught up to "window," the forty tons of aluminum foil strips dropped to confuse its radar. The Germans wouldn't be fooled again. By early last year, when the Royal Air Force returned from Nuremberg, the loss rate was back to one in ten — the same unsustainable number that had led it to build the Lanc in the first place. City raids all but stopped as Bomber Command changed its focus to weakening defenses for D-Day, but now — late March, 1945 — industry and population centres were in the sights again. With Dresden just six weeks ago, moral questions about "area bombing" were finding even Churchill's ear sympathetic.

"You've got to block it out," Joe said. "You've just got to."

Clint lowered his eyes. "Think there'll be orders tomorrow?"

"Don't know," Joe said. "Weather's supposed to be good." He emptied his glass. Any minute, Nellie would be crying, "Time, gents! Finish your drinks!"

—

Nearly back to their bunks, they encountered Mick running toward the mess. "Orders," he panted, exposing his front teeth with the wide gap between them. "Depart base oh-six hundred."

"You had to tell me now, didn't you, Mick?" Joe asked, not for the first time. The Lanc had made her name as a night bomber, but now morning raids were standard.

It was just before eleven when Joe got into his room. He had four hours to sober up and, theoretically, sleep, but nobody slept before a raid. He drank all the water he could hold then crawled into his bunk. He would have preferred being surprised the day-of to staring at the barracks' ceiling all night, thinking about his latest Last Letter to Sheila and their infant son, Harry, written and stowed in his locker to be sent if he didn't return. He put one hand on his chest and another on his stomach, an old trick his mother had taught him to help him relax. He fully expected to be in the same position at reveille.

—

Before a mission, crew members greeted one another with just names, sometimes just nods. They ate together in the mess in virtual silence, each man knowing anything he said could betray his fear. Any man's problem was every man's problem, and no one needed to be reminded: taking twenty-thousand pounds of metal up in the air, plus twice its weight in bombs and fuel, was a battle with simple gravity, let alone enemy flak. Fear was enough to keep Joe and Clint from discussing their headaches, and Joe from letting on that he hadn't slept. He finished his meal and pushed back his chair, making a scraping sound against the floor. Almost in unison, the rest of his table, then the rest of the mess echoed the sound. Joe was among the more experienced skippers; when he made for the briefing, you did too.

—

Fuel loads gave a small hint about a mission, and lately they had been "all tanks full" — long runs into Germany. Black Mike walked in and the men sat up straighter in their chairs. The OC cut an imposing figure, broad-shouldered with a narrow but thick black mustache. Once again, he dramatically lifted the black sheet off the map at the front of the room to unveil Hamburg and its U-boat pens.

The Americans had proven daylight bombing possible with adequate fighter support, and their B-17s were so well-armed they'd even done away with escorts. The Canadians and Brits, on the other hand, worked in gaggles: groups, sometimes as many as ten of them, of a hundred planes organized with fighters wide and bombers protected in the middle. To keep navigation simple, the first gaggle leader trailed a stream of smoke. All the other planes had to do was stay with the group.

Black Mike announced Joe's plane as deputy-lead of the thousand planes, to which Joe said firmly, "Roger, sir." He ranked low for the mission, a Pilot Officer, but didn't doubt for a second that his outfit had earned it. After today, they were due for leave, which was supposed to come every six weeks, but they had climbed the pecking order as other crews had gone down; it had only been three since their last layoff.

"Last thing, men," Black Mike said. "The 262s are finally in combat; as expected, they've got jet engines, and only the best pilots flying 'em. Don't let 'em take you by surprise."

—

The truck ride from hangar to airfield was quieter than breakfast. No one even made eye contact. Joe's bunch stepped out of the back and lit up cigarettes to lengthen the short walk to the plane. In the control van down the runway, the Aldis lamp went green. Hatches opened and men climbed in, began running their checklists: heated gloves and boots, oxygen in the helmets, communications system operational.

Going down was something that only happened to other crews. They had to believe that. They all had their totems: Don wore his junior hockey championship ring; Boss carried the keys to the Pontiac Torpedo his parents had bought him, which he'd only driven a handful of times. Frenchy had one of his girlfriend's stud earrings pinned inside his cap, and Bill had a little doll of his niece's that he'd promised to get back to her. Clint and Mick had never said what they clung to, but neither had denied he had something. Joe always taped the photo of Sheila and baby Harry to Nellie's instrument panel. It was no logical match for the exploding shells from the German eighty-eights, but what was?

Nellie's pumps and gauges looked good; the ground crew hadn't missed anything. Another green flash, and the lead plane's first engine growled to life. Joe nodded to Boss, beside him on the flight deck, who brought the outer starboard motor to life at the same moment as the hundred or so other engineers did, literally shaking the earth beneath them. Boss started the inner next, then the portsides one at a time. It took a moment for all four to synchronize, for their amniotic fluid-like drone to level out, and when it did Joe taxied to the edge of the airstrip and marshalled with the other planes.

Once in position, Joe kissed his fingers and softly brushed his wife and son. This was the real wait — everything ready to go, but unable to take off yet. From here on out, he wasn't a husband, father, or human, but a piece of precision equipment, a gear in an alarm clock set for an exact zero hour: the five-minute window during which, come hell or high water, Nellie had to stay on a steady course for thirty seconds, just long enough for Clint to drop and for her camera to snap a photo.

When the third light came, Joe jumped at the lever and took the plane to top speed. Boss reached over to hold the throttle fully open: it took two men to get a fully loaded Lanc into the sky, and there was always a moment once they were off the ground when Nellie seemed to think a few seconds, to consider giving up and crashing back down. But she got up. Nellie always got up.

—

The climb was steep over the Channel, the course a dogleg over the North Sea. The crew went an hour barely speaking, reassured by the all-encompassing engine noise, the one sound telling them they still hadn't gone down.

"Skip, we've got a problem," Mick's voice broke in from the wireless station.

"Go ahead."

"Lead's made a mistake. The two navigators had different fixes — one visual, the other by radar. They just corrected, but we're all off course."

"Meaning . . . ?"

He heard Mick breathe out, breathe in again. "Some of the fighter cover won't make it in time."

"What do we do?"

"Orders are to proceed to target."

—

Without the error, right about now, the crew would be hearing Clint say, "Target in sight" and going quiet. Then would come the thirty seconds, when the bomb-aimer had to focus, had to ascertain wind direction and speed before letting the payload go. And then finally — *finally* — "Bombs gone" would be heard from the man below, the plane skipping up from the weight drop. Only then could the pilot take his first evasive moves, ditching his false even keel and pulling up, doing whatever it took to get away and leave fighting to the fighters.

## Three Deaths of James Arthur Doole

The target never came into sight today, though. The first gaggle dropped its bombs and turned tail with German fighters roaring up from its fringes. Nellie was already taking fire, flak shells exploding all around.

"We should be over it!" Frenchy yelled from the navigator's station.

All Joe saw below was smoke.

"Clint?" Joe called.

"I can't see it!"

"We've got to go," Boss said.

"Bandits everywhere!" Bill cried. "Got to drop!"

"Clint?" Joe asked again, failing to shove down the panic in his voice.

"I don't know! I don't see — "

Joe looked at Boss again. Boss nodded. "Drop it, Clint," Joe said softly.

"I can't!" he said. "I don't know what — "

"It's down there somewhere," Joe said.

"I can't see — "

More clanging strafe interrupted his protests.

"That's my order, Clint!" Boss screamed. "Drop the fucking bombs!"

Frenchy yelled, "Nine o'clock!"

Joe looked out the right window at a swarm of German planes. Nellie was a sitting duck.

"Bombs gone," Clint muttered.

Joe banked the plane hard left. Don came to life on the tail gun — "Think you got it, Clint" — though surely no one could see through the smoke.

The Lanc levelled.

"Situation, Don?"

No response.

They were taking fire again.

Joe pointed the nose down and jammed the throttle forward, the go-to evasion.

"Talk to me, Don," he said.

Bill responded, frantic. "He's hit, Skipper! I'm on tail gun!"

Frenchy said, "Roger." He would move to mid-upper — they didn't need a navigator now, they needed to get away.

"What do you see, Bill?" Joe asked.

"They're closing — get us out of here!"

"I'm trying!"

Nellie was at top speed.

"They're so fast!" Bill yelled. "There are too many!"

Frenchy added, "They're the new jets!"

"They go down the same!" Joe called. "Keep shooting!"

Joe ducked the plane into what little cloud cover he could find; with a little luck, Nellie might come out the other side all by herself.

The cloud was thin. She popped right out the bottom.

"Six o'clock!" Frenchy yelled. "Bill!"

No reply. The clanging intensified. More shells from the eighty-eights burst around them.

"*Bill?*" Joe called.

Clint left the nose to check the back of the plane.

Mick yelled, "Fire!"

Clint confirmed, "Port! Inner engine!"

In his peripheral vision Joe saw Boss flip the kill switch and hit the engine's fire extinguisher button, not fast enough. An explosion broke the wing. They listed right and began falling.

"Drop what we have, Clint!" Boss yelled.

This time Clint didn't argue. The incendiaries were bound to catch fire, and now was a good time to weigh less. Boss feathered the engines, and Joe deployed flaps. They did everything they knew to do to slow the descent. They were out of the fight. There was a chance they could land the hobbled plane, but just a chance.

Don and Bill were already gone.

"We took a lot of fire," Joe said. "Hard to know if the landing gear will deploy. If not, we'll try to go in on our belly . . . We might make it."

Nellie's drone wasn't what it used to be, but it was still all he could hear — maybe a lullaby. Boss gave the order to the remaining crew: "If you don't want to die without seeing a POW camp, you're free to jump." He looked at Joe. "Personally, I'll take my chances with Skip."

"You're the experts," Clint said. "If you're not jumping, I'm not."

"Me neither," Frenchy said.

They waited for Mick.

"Land this plane, Joe," he finally sniffed.

A crew lived together, Joe thought; a crew waited together. A crew held its breath together when the time came to drop the landing gear. He leaned forward to kiss his wife and son. A crew died together, too.

*Garrett Baxter's short stories have previously appeared in* PEI Online Review, *at LiToronto.com, and elsewhere. "Going Down" is dedicated to his father.*

# Acknowledgements

For publishing versions of stories in this collection, thank you to *Hart House Review, The Nashwaak Review, Paragon, Ottawa Arts Review, The Lion and the Aardvark* (Stone Skin Press), *Little Fiction, The Steel Chisel, BareBack Magazine* and *Hearing Voices: The BareBack Anthology, The Prague Revue* (twice), *Black Heart Magazine, echolocation* (online version), *Riddle Fence, SubTerrain, Partisan* and *Joypuke.*

"Fourfather" was a finalist in the 2014 Writing x Writers contest, judged by Pam Houston, BK Loren and Benjamin Percy. Its prompt was, "Write a story of 250 words or less that features a beetle, a Volkswagen Beetle, or The Beatles."

"Vaporetto" is indebted to the articles "10 Stories We Never Need to See in Workshops Again" by Jon Gingerich and "Three Stories Unlikely to Make It Beyond the Slush Pile" by Joe Hiland. The warning against sleeping with one's students is a paraphrase of something Christopher Hitchens is reported to have said. Information on Venetian water temperatures is courtesy of Justin Kesseler.

"Tender Port" is indebted to Angelique V. Nixon's essay, "Imaginings in/of Paradise: Bahamian Literature and the Culture of a Tourism Economy" (*Anthurium* 8.1).

Personalities and events from the Second World War in "Three Deaths of James Arthur Doole" have been modified for dramatic purposes. The Air Force mission in Part 3, particularly the navigation error that resulted in some of the planes becoming "stragglers," is adapted from an account delivered to the Canadian Aviation Historical Society in Ottawa in 2000 by A.B. (Sandy)

Mutch of the March 31, 1945 bombing of Hamburg. (One evident fictionalization: that the vice-deputy's crew perished.) Other sources for this story include the History Channel's *Battle Stations*, J.L. Granatstein's *The Last Good War*, Air Commodore Johnny Fauquier's November 1945 address to the Empire Club of Canada, and two Reader's Digest books my great-grandmother, Eileen Harnett, gave to me when I was a boy: *The Canadians at War 1939/45* and *The Tools of War 1939/45*. (Thanks, Gram. Love and miss you.) A helpful read was also provided by Bryan Minnes. The cemetery in Part 1 is based on Rusthof Cemetery, Amersfoort, Netherlands, where my own great-grandfather, John Irven Mackenzie, was buried in 1943 after the bomber for which he was navigator was shot down. Family legend has it that he never met his daughter, my paternal grandmother, Jane.

The title "99 Per Cent" is taken from a statement apocryphally attributed to the American Motorcyclist Association, from which outlaw motorcycle clubs' "1%er" designation is said to have been derived.

"Rocky Steps" was presented at Summer Literary Seminars, Vilnius, Lithuania (July 2011), in a workshop led by Josip Novakovich. "Hamburger" and "Be Your Own Master" respectively benefitted from reads by SLS collaborators Jackie Zakrewski and Laurence Levey. "Be Your Own Master" was presented at the inaugural *Catamaran* Writers Conference, Pebble Beach, Calif. (August, 2014), in Gina Ochsner's workshop. Other stories were helpfully read by Nicole Baute and Sarah Simon in a small writing group born of the Toronto Public Library's Writer-in-Residence program in 2012, when Farzana Doctor held the position.

This book's dedication borrows from Antoine de Saint-Exupéry's *Le Petit Prince*, Chapter XV, in which the prince meets a geographer.

Thanks to my editor, Michael Kenyon, whose steady hand and inspired suggestions greatly improved these stories, and to Al and Jackie Forrie and Thistledown Press for bringing this book into the world; to Richard Scarsbrook, my mentor at George Brown College, who believes in every one of his students, as well as Patricia Westerhof, Andrew F. Sullivan, and Amanda Leduc, for kindly introducing me to their readers; to the F&G Writers Group (Susan Alexander, Julie McArthur, Nadia Ragbar, Robert Shaw, and Brad Weber), which read several of these stories before anyone else did; to the many friends who read my very earliest drafts and encouraged me to keep writing; to the editors who've provided humane rejections or other counsel, and to the reading series and other literary events that have welcomed me and my work, especially the Brockton Writers Series community — collaborators, readers, and friends who lift my spirits and a whole neighbourhood every eight weeks.

*Surtout, merci à mon petit chat*, Pauline.